THE
⚔ DOLL ⚔
GRAVEYARD

THE
DOLL
GRAVEYARD

LOIS RUBY

SCHOLASTIC INC.

HAUNTINGS

No part of this publication may be reproduced, stored in a retrieval system, or transmitted in any form or by any means, electronic, mechanical, photocopying, recording, or otherwise, without written permission of the publisher. For information regarding permission, write to Scholastic Inc., Attention: Permissions Department, 557 Broadway, New York, NY 10012.

ISBN 978-0-545-61786-4

12 11 10 9 8 7 6 5 4 3 2 1   14 15 16 17 18 19/0

Printed in the U.S.A.   40
First printing, July 2014

Designed by Whitney Lyle

IN MEMORY OF ROGER JAY RUBY
FOR HIS UNDYING SUPPORT

CHAPTER ONE

THE TRUTH CAN BE TRICKY. IN ALL MY TWELVE years I've never lied. Well, actually I won't be twelve until next month. Okay, to be honest, I sometimes exaggerate a little, and maybe I'll hold back a few details, but that's because I keep getting in trouble for telling the whole truth. Mom says I think with my mouth. Like, last week, Evvie and I rode our bikes to Melissa's sleepover, and when we got there, all sweaty, Evvie said, "Yeeks, I must smell like a pig," and I said, "Pigs don't sweat. You smell like a goat." It was the truth, but she didn't speak to me all night.

Speaking of speaking, my annoying brother, Brian, who's nine, hangs on to words like they're shiny quarters, too valuable to spend, especially now that our lives have been turned upside down. I stomp around and yell, but he just holds it all in. That can't be good, can it? If I stuck him with a pin, he'd pop like a balloon.

Right now Mom and I are cleaning the living room, or more like she's cleaning and I'm batting around a feather duster. "It makes me mad that I can't get Brian talking when there's so much to say about Dad and all that stuff."

"Give him time, Shelby," Mom says, turning off the vacuum.

"Mom!" She'd never admit it, but Brian is her favorite. She always makes excuses for him. "Would it kill him to say what's on his mind?" I demand.

Mom sighs. She's out of the crying phase of their divorce and into the deep-sighing phase now. "Yes, Shelby, it would kill him. Not literally, but there's a lot in his heart, and it's too painful for him to talk about it."

"He'd feel better if he got it out. It's the healthy thing to do." I'm practically barking at my poor mom, but I can't stop.

"That's the difference between the two of you, honey. You get white-hot mad, and he freezes. You're so much like your father," she says under her breath as Brian comes into the living room. She hands him a dustrag and a can of Pledge.

"This?" He points to the coffee table.

2

See what I mean? He could have said, "Okay, I guess you want me to dust this table. I'd be glad to, Mom." But he says it all in one word and a question mark.

"Yes, and we want to finish up quickly to get to the hospital. Aunt Amelia's expecting us," Mom says.

"Ugh. We just saw her Thursday," I mutter, and now we have to spend a perfectly beautiful August afternoon at St. Catherine's Hospital with creaky old Aunt Amelia. Did anyone ask me what I wanted to do this afternoon? Of course not. Does anyone ever? "You don't want to go, do you, Brian?"

"Nope."

Wrapping the cord around the vacuum, Mom promises, "It'll just be a short visit. She loves seeing you kids."

Brian pulls at the fringe on his cutoff shorts and says, "Seems like she's already dead."

"Mom, did you hear that? A whole sentence!" Well, this calls for a celebration. Like a crazed bird, I chirp, "Come on, Brian, let's go outside and pick some flowers to take to Aunt Amelia."

He shrugs and follows me out to the yard, where I pick a bunch of daisies.

"Mad at the flowers?" Brian asks.

"No, why are you asking me that?"

He demonstrates a ferocious yank, like rescuing a drowning swimmer.

He's right — it's not the flowers' fault. And he's right about old Aunt Amelia, too. There's something creepy about her. For one thing, she never smiles. Maybe it's because her false teeth might fall out. She's older than the earth's crust, at least eighty-six. She's not actually my aunt, she's Mom's, because she's Gram's older sister. But she's a sourpuss and not at all like my sweet grandma, who passed away when I was nine. How come the sour ones live longer, just the way pickles last forever, but sweet cucumbers turn mushy in the veggie bin?

Dad doesn't like her much, either, but he used to say, "Be patient with the old girl, Shel. She's got one foot in the grave."

I wonder when the other foot will follow.

Aunt Amelia's hospital room is hot enough to boil lobsters. She's shrunk to the size of a withered old child, and the hospital bed looks hugely white around her. Mom plants a kiss on her walnut face, but I'm not about to do

that, because she smells like vitamins, which I hate, especially the big ones that get stuck going down.

"Hand me my glasses, Shelby Constance," she says in
her raspy old voice, "so I can better see your face." As if
she could see much at all. Her eyes are dim and cloudy.
Mom says she's afraid to have cataract surgery.

I ease the glasses onto her nose, and one spidery hand
comes out of the covers to straighten them. "Ah, yes.
Don't let that frown freeze on your face," she warns.
"Where's the boy?"

Mom hustles Brian to the bedside. He smiles and
hands over the daisies when Mom pokes his side.

"Daisies. Hmph. Smell like feet, if you ask me. Stick
that bunch in my water pitcher." She squints to give
Brian a good look. "Not very tall, are you?"

"He's only nine," I remind her, because Brian's
sensitive about his size, which is just right . . . for a
seven-year-old.

"Now listen here," Aunt Amelia says, and we all huddle
close as though she's about to make a big announcement,
which she does. "I'm not going to be around much
longer. . . ."

Mom hushes her.

"Be sensible, Serena. My show's had a long run, but the curtain is about to drop with a quiet thud."

Brian flashes me a *What's she saying?* look, and I shrug *Who knows?*

"It's about the house at Cinder Creek."

She means that ugly old rambling monstrosity in front of her little cottage. We've never actually been in it, but just passing it is chilling enough, because every window looks painted shut, and inside I can see nothing but dark air. The house leans a little, too, as though it'll topple over if a big wind howls through the property.

"What about the house?" Mom patiently asks, dabbing at some drool at the corner of Aunt Amelia's mouth.

Turning toward her bedside table seems to take every ounce of strength Aunt Amelia can call up, but she reaches into the drawer and pulls out a key on a coiled stretchy thing and hands it to Mom. "It's yours."

"The key? What for?"

"The key is just a *key*," Aunt Amelia snaps. "What's important is that it opens the front door. Of the house. Which is yours."

Mom protests, "It's not mine. It's not even your house."

"Oh, but it is, Serena. I just never said. Old Mr. Thornewood's will deeded it to me at the turn of this century. I've just rented it out to unsuspecting people."

"Then why did you stay in that funny little cottage?" I blurt out.

"The big house is a place for families to dwell in, and not very happily up to this point, I might add. All those ill-spirited, spoiled girls. You'll change that, Shelby Constance."

"I will? How?"

"With kindness," she spits out irritably. "You'll tie up loose ends," but she never explains what those loose ends are. "You children have been through too much these past months. You need a distraction — a game, if you will. I've set up an interesting situation for you to remember me by. You're bright enough to figure it all out, you and the boy. As for me, I've had all I want of that house and its unsavory history. Now, the cottage is a different story. It is my home. Was. I won't be going back there."

The key jingles from Mom's wrist. "Don't be silly. I'll take you home with me until you're feeling strong enough to return to the cottage."

"You are *not* listening to me!" Aunt Amelia rasps.

Just then, a nurse comes in, gloved in purple and pointing a syringe. "Time for your antibiotic injection, Miss Stanhope."

Aunt Amelia waves her away. "No need to stick a fork in me to see if I'm done. I can tell you flat out, I'm overdone."

"Could you come back in a few minutes?" Mom asks, and the nurse hurls her latex gloves in the trash and kicks the door closed behind her.

"She's unfit to serve the ailing," Aunt Amelia mutters. "As I was saying, the paperwork is done, the house is now yours, Serena."

"We already have our own house," I protest.

Ignoring me, Aunt Amelia continues, "Now, Serena, hear me: You're in need of a change to get away from that scoundrel who left you high and dry."

By *scoundrel*, she means Dad. She's almost as mad at him as I am, and suddenly I like her better.

"The house is just the thing for you and Shelby Constance and, what's your name, boy?"

"Bradley," Brian says, and I nearly crack up.

"Ah, yes, Bradley, like the great general."

"I expect you'll move into the house shortly after I'm planted in a muddy grave at Gates of Eternal Oblivion."

"Let's talk about your getting well," Mom insists, grasping Aunt Amelia's hand, which is dotted with brown age spots.

"Oh, piffle!" Aunt Amelia slides her hand away and kneads it with her other hand. I think her bones hurt. "Now, one word of warning, Serena: Don't let those fool television people into the house."

My ears perk up. "What television people, Aunt Amelia?"

"Pushy producers from some cable station. They've got their greedy eyes on the house for one of those ludicrous reality shows, *America's Most Amazing*. Cinder Creek has some history, all right, but it's nobody's business but yours now, and Shelby Constance, mark my words: It's up to you to fit all the pieces together."

"What pieces, Aunt Amelia?" I hate jigsaw puzzles. And now I've got puzzle pieces and loose ends and no clue as to what she's talking about.

"Those television people pestered me all last month about it, but don't you give in, hear, Serena? Consider it my dying wish."

Mom starts to say, "No more talk about —" but I interrupt with a startling question:

"What's so special about the house that *America's Most Amazing* is interested?" More loose ends?

Aunt Amelia presses her thin white lips together and refuses to answer, which only makes me more curious, not to mention mad. Then she reaches under her pillow and pulls out an envelope for Mom. "Enough in here for you to start that computer soup business you've been nattering on about."

Mom's eyebrows shoot up. SerenaStockPot.com has been her dream for years, but there's never been the money to make it come true.

"Aunt Amelia, I can't . . ."

"Nonsense. You're my only living relative."

What about Brian and me? Aren't we alive?

"Am I to take a fistful of money to my grave for the worms to chew on?" Aunt Amelia pats Mom's hand. "Now, there's just one small detail about the house: He's called Canto Caliberti. Well, that's his theatrical name, not his Christian, given name. He's the new owner of my cottage, which he'll be occupying from now until they carry him out in a box. It shouldn't be long. Lord, the man's even older than I am." She goes into a coughing fit, holding the sheet up to her lips, and when she settles down, she says, "General Bradley, come here." Brian steps forward, but not too close. "You too, Shelby Constance." I elbow Brian out of the way so I can be in front. Just a big-sister habit, I guess.

"Children have been my life and work, teaching the little rascals, though I thank the good Lord I never had to put up with any of my own. I have a gift for you. Lean in," she commands, and I do, holding my breath against the vitamin smell. Ugh. "This is my gift: Don't be too picky about loving someone, understand?"

"Hunh-uh," Brian says, rearing back.

"You will, in the fullness of time." Her hand slides under her pillow again, and she pulls out a floppy gold-colored lacy thing about the size of a dinner plate. She thrusts it into my hands. "Don't lose it, Shelby Constance."

"I won't, but what is it?" I turn it over and see that it's got a center indentation about three inches across. "Oh, is it a hat?"

"Clever child. A hat precisely. It belongs to Isabella."

"Whoever Isabella is, she must have a very small head and an even smaller brain."

Aunt Amelia wrinkles her brow; I can't believe it

could be any more wrinkled than it already was. "Small head and no brain a'tall. Isabella is a doll."

I'm about to blurt something out, like, "Why on earth are you giving me a doll's hat when there's no doll under it?" but Mom's look freezes the words on my tongue.

"Miss Isabella has many friends, ·Shelby Constance. You'll meet them. Lord knows we all need friends in high places. Tuck that thought into your mind."

I just nod, but the thought in my mind is, *I hope I never get this old and weird.*

"And for General Bradley?" Once again she pulls a treasure out from under her pillow — a huge, fancy pipe. "Yours," she says, thrusting it into Brian's hand.

It rattles when he turns it over. He's got to be wondering what he's supposed to do with an old pipe. It's got a very long, curvy stem with a gold braid tassel hanging from it, and a deep porcelain barrel that's hinged.

" 'Twas Mr. Thornewood's pipe, a gift from the king of Sweden. Ceremonial, not for smoking. I do so love the scent of fresh tobacco," she says dreamily. "Up until this pneumonia bout, I smoked a pipe myself, you know."

Just thinking of Aunt Amelia puffing away is hilarious, and I don't dare look at Brian, who's got his hand clasped over his mouth to keep from snorting out a laugh.

"Are you a chess player, General Bradley?" asks Aunt Amelia.

"Yes, ma'am." Finally she's speaking his language.

"Good, fine. I never cottoned to the game, though Canto did his best to teach me. He's a grand master or some such rubbish. Now scat, all of you, or you're going to witness something you'll wish you hadn't."

Mom leans in to kiss our old aunt again. "Rest in peace," Mom says, tears filling her eyes.

"I expect," Aunt Amelia replies.

CHAPTER TWO

WE'RE AT YOGURTPALOOZA, WHERE YOU PUMP your own yogurt into the trough size of your choice. I'm suspicious because Mom hasn't said a word about all the super-sugary toppings we glopped on. Uh-oh. I was right.

"Aunt Amelia has given us a wonderful gift," Mom says. "A new start on life."

"*Mom!* You're not seriously thinking of moving us to that house in Cinder Creek, are you?"

She sucks butterscotch off her spoon and gazes up at the swirling fan. She *is* seriously thinking about it! "We really need to move, kids."

"No, we don't!" It's not the first time she's said it, but this time there's an affordable way to do it. I beat my spoon on the metal table. "Our house is perfect for us, whether *he* lives there or not."

He hasn't lived with us since April first. April Fools' Day. Ha! That's the day Brian came home from soccer — not that the little twerp's a great athlete — and said he'd seen Dad across the street from Ramblers, where the team went for Cokes after practice.

"You must be mistaken," Mom said that awful day. "Your father's at market in North Carolina buying for the furniture store. You know that, Brian."

Brian raised his chin in the air. It's his *I mean business* look. "Is not. He was across the street from Ramblers, and he was pulling some lady by the hand."

Mom turned white, then greenish. "Brian Tate, are you lying?"

Brian held up his fingers in a V. "Cub Scout's honor, Mom, honest."

The beginning of the end.

Mom's name is Serena. Dad's is Sam. All my life it's been Serena-and-Sam, run together like they had one name. But now it's Sam-and-Terri-and-Marcus, Terri's son, who's Brian's age. I'm furious about it, and that's the truth. You would be, too. I've got hazel eyes, and when I'm mad they shoot daggers at people. Gram used to say, "Shelby Constance, you have the personality of a curly-haired, fiery redhead. How did you ever end up with that lovely brown hair, straight as rain?" Okay, Gram was a little biased.

Brian's the one with the curly hair and curly eyelashes that are wasted on a boy, and the coppery hair like Dad's.

Dad who? Oh, yeah, the man with the *other family*.

Once Dad had all his things out of the basement, including his tackle box and fishing rod from when we used to go to Horsetooth Reservoir together every Memorial Day weekend, the big question that'd been hanging over us was, *What's next?* Now I know.

Yogurtpalooza is filling with teenagers on summer vacation, laughing and fist-bumping, not a care in the world, while my world is collapsing all around me. It *so* isn't fair.

"We need to get out of Denver," Mom says. "Too many memories here."

Brian keeps quiet, as usual, and just picks at the drizzles on his yogurt. So I drag him into the argument. "You don't want to move, do you, Brian?" He grunts, which gives me something to jump on. "See? He doesn't, either. Come on, Mom, it's not like we're going to run into Terri when we go to Walmart to get TP, I mean, *really*, Denver's a big city."

Mom's sigh shakes her whole face. "It's a small world after all."

Which reminds me of last summer when the four of us went to Disney World.

That'll never happen again.

Two weeks after Aunt Amelia's funeral, our house has a SOLD sign in the front yard. If it would do me any good to plant myself on the front steps and refuse to go, I would. But it's hopeless. We're packed, and our voices echo all over the empty house as the last of our things are loaded into a U-Haul tethered to our car.

Brian sits up front with Mom; I sulk in the backseat with Chester, our chocolate Lab, who seems really excited about all this change. *He* doesn't have to leave his friends and go to a new school. I lean forward and practically shout in Mom's ear, "Chester is the only one who's happy about this move, Mom. I hope you know that."

"You've been clear on that point," Mom says, glaring at me in the rearview mirror.

It's an endless two hundred miles to Cinder Creek. Mom's run through all of the songs on the playlist she made for the drive, and the car's filled with a stony silence. Too much time to think.

Cinder Creek, Colorado. Not even a real place. I was embarrassed to tell Evvie and Melissa that it's just an abandoned coal-mining town north of the dinky city of Trinidad. It's where all the coal-company bigwigs lived way back *when*. Aunt Amelia once told us that Mr. Thornewood owned a small coal mine that didn't produce much coal, but he didn't care, because he struck oil instead. She showed us a yellowed newspaper from 1929 with the headline *THORNEWOOD TURNS KING COAL INTO BLACK GOLD*.

So I guess he built that huge house just to show everybody he was stinking rich. The absolutely only good thing about this move is the promise of *America's Most Amazing*.

My heart clenches as Mom pulls into the winding driveway that leads to our house and two others way up a hill. The minute the car doors open, Chester bounds out, Brian right behind him. Just Mom and me left in the sweltering car. The air-conditioning hasn't worked since Dad left.

Wiping sweat off her forehead, she says, "It's a nice house, isn't it? We'll be okay here, you'll see. The change

will be good for all of us. It'll get us far away from . . ."
Lately we've both talked a lot in unfinished sentences,
and I know just what she means. Away from Dad, away
from the *other family*.

I miss Dad like mad. In fact, *mad* says it all.

"You'll start to feel at home in time," Mom assures
me as she jiggles the house keys.

"Never," I snarl. I get out and slam the car door so
hard that the window rattles.

CHAPTER THREE

THE FRONT DOOR MUST HAVE SWELLED OR warped in the heat. It creaks and scrapes across the floor inside, leaving a white swath in the wood.

Typical of chocolate Labs everywhere, Chester makes himself right at home. He trots into the dark front parlor and sniffs under the circle of couches.

"I'll leave the door open," Mom says, swatting giant flies away. "It smells a little musty."

A little? Like a raccoon died in here a long time ago.

Brian runs to the stairs. "First pick of rooms."

"No fair. I'm the oldest," I mutter, but he's already upstairs.

Mom tiptoes around, turning on lamps to brighten the gloom, plumping couch pillows, poking at ash in the fireplace. "Chester! Off the couch! I just love this gorgeous coffee table." The huge round table sits in the middle of the three kidney-shaped, faded green velvet couches. "Don't sit on the table like you did at home. Well, I mean, where we used to live. This is home now. The beveled glass top could easily break. Oh, and look at the giant tapestry hanging over there. What fantastic needlework detail in that fox-hunt scene. It makes me feel like we're living in a castle."

"It's super ugly," I grumble. So's the awful portrait hanging over the fireplace. It's a huge picture of a woman staring straight ahead, only she has a black net veil over her nose and mouth. She has broad shoulders, and her eyes are extra large, like someone just came up behind her and yelled "Boo!"

"It's probably Mrs. Thornewood," Mom observes. "I'm surprised the recent tenants didn't take the portrait down. I'd take it down if I weren't so skittish about heights."

"If Dad were here . . ." Of course, I don't complete that thought.

Blowing her bangs off her forehead, Mom says, "Try to put a little positive energy into this adventure, Shelby."

Brian comes barreling down the stairs. "My room's got a desk with cubbyholes for *Star Wars* guys. Come see?"

I'm much more interested in that round table and what's under the glass that rests about three inches over the wood part. It's like a giant shadow box.

Mom wanders out of the room, and I hear her shout, "This kitchen is fabulous!" She's opening and slamming cabinets and drawers. "So well designed!"

She'll be in there awhile, kissing all the appliances, so I lift the glass top and blow dust off the pieces of doll-house furniture that Aunt Amelia, or whoever, had randomly plunked down under there. The spindly little legs of three chairs huddle around a kitchen table that's carved with lots of curlicues and covered in a blue-and-white-checkered cloth the size of a postage stamp. Nearby hulks an oven with a black stovepipe, and a pair of floor lamps with pink-fringed shades that seem to be guarding all these odd pieces. A four-poster bed draped in a gauzy mosquito net looks isolated off in a corner. A figure under the gauze draws my eyes, so I lift the netting; who wouldn't? Lying on a yellowed flannel sheet is a doll the size of my thumb. Suddenly her eyes click open!

Brian jumps. "How'd she do that?"

"I jiggled the bed, that's all." Two tiny licorice

circles look straight up at me. Then her eyelids drift closed, shutting me out and leaving me feeling curiously snubbed, like when Evvie and Melissa whisper secrets to each other.

Then the sun slides behind a cloud, and the room turns even gloomier. That tapestry nearly covers one wall in grim tones of brown and sickly green, soaking up what little light is left.

Brian's standing in front of the portrait that seems to be Mrs. Thornewood. The frame is gaudy gold and black, as if somebody went postal with a carving knife. Brian's sneaking peeks at it and fiddling with the tiny chess pieces. The set is on a small round table in front of the giant portrait.

"Chess set's funky," he reports, then suddenly bubbles over with words. "Look at it. The pieces are way small, and they don't just slide on the table. They've got holes at the bottom so they fit onto pegs on the chessboard. Can't move the board, either. It's glued to the table." Brian absently snaps pieces on and off the pegs while staring at the painting of Mrs. Thornewood. "How come half her face is covered with that black net stuff?" he asks. "It's like a mask."

I try to see it through his eyes, and that's when I notice that it's not a flat painting at all. It's a picture made of paper cuttings. Some of it is deeper, and some of it sticks out farther. It's three-dimensional.

"I dunno. Maybe she's grotesque — three noses or black teeth, hairy warts, or she has a beard."

Brian wrinkles his freckly nose at the portrait. "Or maybe she's hiding something. Don't you wish we could yank that mask down?"

"No way! Who wants to see warts with wiry hairs springing from them?"

"If you don't put the glass down, Mom's gonna catch you," Brian teases.

Mr. Goody Two-Shoes is always looking for ways to get me in trouble, because he knows I'll do the opposite of what he says, but at least he's talking! And then I glance up at the hairy-wart lady and see that her eyes are really odd, since they're the only thing we see of her face. In fact, her eyes seem to be following me. "Watch this, Brian." When I shift to my left side, her eyes go that way. I squat down, and her eyes lower. It's like they're magnetized. "Maybe that's one of the things *America's Most Amazing* is interested in. It would be cool to have our house on TV."

"Maybe," Brian says doubtfully. Sometimes I think my brother was born a stodgy old man. "How'd the artist do that? Make the eyes go wherever you go?"

"Who knows?"

"Creeps me out. Not looking at it ever again," he mutters, but of course he can't resist and he glances up at it out of the corner of his eye. "I'm sticking to chess." *Click, click,* Brian snaps the pawns and rooks onto the pegs. "Hey, one's missing. No fun playing when the queen's gone."

"Oh, who cares? I don't want to play chess anyway." Believe me, it drives me crazy when Brian beats me nine games out of ten, especially since Dad taught us both at the same time.

The whole room feels dark and forbidding now, creepy even with the stained-glass lamps throwing their tongue-pink glow. I quickly lay the glass top back on the table and give that strange doll one last glance. Her eyes have snapped open again, and they stay open no matter how much I shake the table. I'd swear she doesn't want to be stuck inside there.

Ridiculous. Tiny dolls don't *want* anything. But her eyes seem almost pleading.

How can something smaller than a Snickers bar make me feel so jumpy?

News flash: Like I told Mom, this house will never be home, and I don't want to spend one more day here.

But what choice do I have? I'm stuck just like that doll inside the table.

CHAPTER FOUR

THE LAST BOX IS OUT OF THE U-HAUL. MOM'S unpacking the kitchen and has cornered Brian into helping her line shelves. All I want to do is go soak in a tub of bubble bath, but first, here comes a girl up the front steps carrying a pie flat on the palm of her hand. I hope it's apricot or rhubarb, just please, not coconut cream.

"I'm Mariah O'Donnell. That's Ma-RYE-uh, not Maria," the girl says, handing me the pie, which is as heavy as a bucket of nails. "My mother said to bring it; it's what neighbors do. It's beefsteak-and-kidney pie, an O'Donnell family specialty."

Ugh! I try not to let my face sag with disappointment.

"Mother made me bring a pie for the last family, too. The one with that girl Emily. What's your name?" she asks flatly, like she doesn't care whether my name's Shelby or Bongo.

"Shelby. My brother's Brian. He's nine. Are you and I in the same grade?" At least I'll know *someone* in my new school.

"Mother homeschools me," Mariah says, shifting from foot to foot.

Will there be nothing but disappointments here in Cinder Creek? She just stands there, barely blinking, then says, "It's a tradition, bringing pies to this house. We did it for every one of the tenants. Grandmother Truva brought one for the first people here, the Thornewoods. They had a daughter called Sadie. Mean as a Tasmanian she-devil, that's what Grandmother Truva said."

Mariah-not-Maria sure isn't the warm, fuzzy type, but I try to be nice. "Tell me about the last girl who lived here, Emily. Were you friends with her?"

"Are you kidding?" There's an awkward pause that leaves me full of questions. "She's about my age, same as Sadie, same as you. You're twelvish? I'm eleven, but I'm big-boned."

I'll say. She's practically a foot taller than I am, and her colorless nest of tight curls looks like it's trying to escape from the wild knot on top of her head. It makes her look about six feet tall.

"Emily was loopy," says Mariah, spinning her finger in little circles at the side of her head.

"You mean crazy?" Now I'm hooked. "What kind of crazy?"

"Mother says not to gossip." Those are her words, but I can see that she's dying to spill it all.

"It's not gossip if it's about the history of my house. It's research." The pie is getting heavier by the minute, and I'm holding it in both hands, wondering how many kidneys are in it, and whose.

"Okay, research. It's about why they moved, the Smythes. So they could lock Emily up in a crazy ward in Denver. She heard voices, saw things that weren't there. See? Nutso."

Is nutso Emily the one who trapped that teeny doll under the glass? Because Emily saw and heard things that weren't really happening? But that little doll *did* give me the creepy-crawlies with her staring eyes that snapped open and wouldn't close, and I'm not a bit crazy. I guess I'd better find out a lot more about Emily Smythe.

"Which one of those is yours, Mariah?" I motion toward the two grim houses that huddle together up the hill.

She lets out an indignant puff. "We're in the Keystone Duplexes a half mile up the road. No way we'd live *here*."

Boy, that's reassuring! "Do you know who *does* live in those two houses? I haven't seen anyone coming or going."

"Empty, both of 'em. Last tenants left just before you moved in. Only stayed about a week. Can't help wondering what spooked 'em out so fast."

"You mean we're all alone out here?"

"You got it. There's that rickety cottage behind your house, but I heard the old lady croaked."

"That old lady was my great-aunt Amelia," I snap.

"Sorry for your loss," she says, not sounding a bit sorry. "Yeah, Old Man Thornewood built all three houses plus the cottage. When he died, he left the other two to some bank in Denver. They rent 'em out every year or two, but nobody stays long. Who wants to live in a drafty old house with ghosts and ghouls?"

"You're telling me they're haunted?"

Mariah shrugs. "Way back from the coal-mining days, last century. That's what Grandmother Truva used to say before she left this world a few years ago."

"Sorry for your loss," I echo, in the same dull tone Mariah used.

"Nothin' to be sorry about. Anyway, I don't believe the haunted thing for a second. Course, I wouldn't care to spend a dark, thunderous night in one of 'em, would you? Wind howling like a coyote?" We both look up the hill toward the pair of matching houses that seem to lean toward each other, with just a narrow walkway between them. All the windows are shuttered except one on the third floor of the house on the right, where a thin curtain billows out. Why is the window open if no one lives there?

"Anyway, electricity and heat's turned off, so you'd freeze your innards if you stayed there. I like my innards warm. It's been known to get thirty below out here, in wintertime."

Suddenly I feel chilled as a sweeping breeze cools my sweaty body, and I realize that there's not much out here to shelter us from the wind. "Want to come in? We're not unpacked yet, and my room's a holy mess."

"Nope."

What a peculiar girl. She doesn't even make up an excuse. Just "Nope," and she keeps standing there waiting for . . . what? Am I supposed to tip her for delivering the awful pie?

She scrapes her sneakers on the welcome mat a few times, then about-faces and starts down the stairs, muttering in her gravelly voice, "You sure know how to pick a neighborhood."

CHAPTER FIVE

"A SIX-BURNER STOVE!" MOM'S STILL WIGGING out on kitchen appliances. "A side-by-side freezer/fridge, and enough granite-slab counter space to do surgery."

Wow, you could get your appendix out while you wait for a baked potato. Personally, I don't care about kitchens. I'm moving right into the upstairs bathroom, since my own room is all red flocked wallpaper and a spindly, narrow bed with sagging springs that squeal every time you move an inch. Was this Emily Smythe's bedroom?

It must have been Emily's family who had the good sense to update the prehistoric bathrooms and kitchen in this creepy old house. Gram would have said they're to die for. Every muscle in my whole body is achy from pushing furniture around and hauling boxes up the stairs, not to mention hefting that kidney pie, so I lock myself and Chester in the bathroom and fill up the huge triangular tub with hot water and about a quart of bubble bath. It nearly overflows when I sink into the water up to my shoulders and let my hands and feet float like they're weightless ghosts riding the bubbles and gentle waves. I can just feel stings of anger seeping out of me into the warm water.

Chester's chomping to jump into the tub with me, but then it *would* overflow, and chocolate-brown dog hair would clog the fancy new plumbing, so I tell him, "Hang on, pup. I'll take you out for a run later, okay?"

He whips his tail around, then coils onto the bath mat and snoozes patiently.

Not Brian. He's banging on the bathroom door. "I gotta go. It's an emergency!"

What a colossal pest. "There's a bathroom downstairs, Brian. It's the little room with the weird wallpaper that looks like old Sunday funnies. Oh, and it has a toilet. You can't miss it." Finally I hear his footsteps stomping down the creaky stairs, but in two minutes he's back pounding on the door.

"Come on, Shelby. Mom says to take boxes up to the attic."

"Go ahead," I say lazily.

"Hunh-uh, not alone!"

"Okaaaay. Give me ten minutes, and we'll do the attic thing." Chester raises one ear in agreement that we'll just keep the pest waiting a lot longer.

I've never lived in a house with an attic, and this one is the kind you have to move a rickety ladder up to, then slide the ceiling trapdoor aside and hoist yourself up onto the attic floor. Now I wish I hadn't. It's dark and smells like soured milk up here. I try to scramble to my feet till my head hits the ceiling. You'd have to be about the size of a shrunken Pygmy to stand up. That pink insulation fluff stuff sticks out between the wall slats. There's a small round window like the porthole on a ship, which gives a circle of light to the big, dark space that spans the whole length of the second floor of the house. Somehow that little bit of sunshine makes everything seem spookier, lighting up dust motes that swirl, though there's not a breath of a breeze. I think the air up here's stood still for about a hundred years.

Brian hands a bunch of flattened cartons up to me, and I slide them across the bare plank floor. The attic seems to be totally empty, but then one of the cartons sails across the floor and thuds into something with a peaked roof jutting up in the shadow. A dollhouse.

"Come up here, Brian." He scuttles up behind me, and we crawl over and push the little house across the floor toward the porthole for a better look.

I ask, "Does this look familiar to you?"

"Kind of."

"Look here. Two windows with pale green lace curtains on each side of the front door. Four steps up, then a flat landing, then six more steps to the blue door. It's just like our house, even down to the goat-shaped knocker on the blue door."

"Same furniture inside, too. Cool."

Now I see the three green velvet couches circling the beveled glass-top table in the front parlor. Somebody built this dollhouse as an exact copy of the big house. Probably Mr. Thornewood built it for Sadie, the Tasmanian she-devil Mariah told me about.

The little house looks so lonely and abandoned. I wonder why Emily, or any of the other tenants, didn't take it with them when they moved.

Brian asks, "Where are the people?"

Good question. There's a mess on the floor, and the sink's full of those teeny dishes and pots and pans. It

36

looks like everybody took off in a hurry. My eyes roam around the two stories of the house. "At least they didn't forget to take the baby, see? The crib's empty."

Brian chuckles. "Old-time toilet with the thing you pull instead of flush!"

"Not like our bathrooms, thank goodness. This dollhouse was probably built way back in the last century, and no one bothered to remodel it."

"Bathtub has claws, see?" Brian reaches in and pulls out the old-fashioned oval tub, then shoves it back in the dollhouse with a gasp.

"What? WHAT?" I yell.

He points to the bathtub. A tiny doll is floating facedown in a small puddle of water. Brian whispers, "They didn't take the baby."

"Let's get out of here." We both slide across the floor and scamper down the ladder super quick, then glide down the smooth banister to the ground floor, landing on a Persian rug that covers the hardwood. Chester's waiting for us. "Outside, both of you," I command. "It was stifling up there; we need fresh air." Brian tears out the front door, Chester right behind him, and I walk slowly, wondering if Sadie loved her dollhouse. I'm also wondering what kind of a kid would drown a baby in the bathtub. Crazy Emily?

Outside, I look up at dark thunderclouds rolling in. "We won't have much time out here before the rain starts. So enjoy it while it lasts."

The yard seems to be acres wide, but not much deeper than the house, and most of it is overgrown with weeds and tall grass. The only thing that saves it from being flat, ugly land are the twin mountains, the Spanish Peaks, dotting the horizon off in the distance. I'll bet they look really pretty dusted with snow. Something to look forward to, since we seem to be trapped here forever.

We pass a small fishing hole on the north side where no fish could survive in the mustard-yellow algae, and I think about fishing with Dad at Horsetooth Reservoir. *Don't go there*, I remind myself. *You're here, now . . .* where lots of weeping willow branches sag from the trees and brush the ground. The air is usually hot and still in late August, but those storm clouds are rolling in. There's a grassy clearing between two trees where someone seems to have chopped off the low-hanging branches. It looks strange in the middle of all that growth of weeds and grass and weeping willows. Chester sniffs the ground and whimpers. Maybe there's a juicy bone buried under there that he hasn't got the heart to go for right now, which is shocking, because Chester's a great digger.

So Brian and I move in closer to see what's stopped him. Chills ripple up and down my spine.

It's a graveyard, a miniature cemetery with five tiny wooden markers close together in a horseshoe shape, and one larger one set way apart, as if someone didn't want that body buried with the rest.

CHAPTER SIX

WHATEVER'S BURIED HERE HAS TO BE REALLY small, maybe goldfish or pet mice or hamsters, because the whole horseshoe space is only about two feet for the five graves. Someone scribbled messy names on those wooden sticks with a Sharpie, like they were in a huge hurry to get these dead things underground. Same as the doll people who were in a hurry to get out of the house in the attic. What's everybody's rush?

A huge question hits me: Who-what-where-when-why? Oops, that's five questions, the biggie being, *What's buried here?*

Five of the wooden grave markers look like those tongue depressors you gag on when doctors look down your throat. One says *Dotty Woman*, with *C.B.* nestled between *Betsy Anne* and *Baby Daisy*. I'm startled to see a marker for *Miss Amelia*. It can't be a coincidence.

"Aunt Amelia?" Brian asks, wide-eyed.

"Hardly. She's buried in Denver, and besides, even if they shrink-wrapped her, she wouldn't fit in this grave." Who *are* these creatures, Betsy Anne and C.B. and all? They don't sound like names for goldfish or hamsters.

Brian manages a breathless, "Wow."

I couldn't have said it better myself.

The sixth grave has a larger marker about a foot high and rounded on top like a more traditional gravestone. It says *LADY R.I.P.* Lady sounds like a good name for a dog, but why is this grave separated from the others?

Now Chester begins rooting around in the little cemetery.

"Don't, pup," I command, pulling him away by his collar, but he goes right back to the Miss Amelia marker and frantically pulls at the grass and dirt with one front paw after the other, like he's pedaling a bike, until his claws click against something. He tosses out dirt and clamps his teeth around a small doll, only about five inches tall. Chester drops her at my feet. Miss Amelia. Matted hair sticks out of her head in black clumps, and she has hard, dark eyes too big for her delicate face. And no eyelids.

So, they're dolls, Baby Daisy and the rest? Like the one under the glass-top table, only bigger? Brian's holding

Miss Amelia upside down by one black high-laced shoe. Her thick black wool dress hangs over her hair, but old-fashioned muslin pantaloons modestly cover her. I grab her away from Brian and turn her right side up. Her face is cracked and dotted with black flecks and pinholes. Her lips twist in a zigzag, as if the doll maker molded a grotesque mouth when the clay was soft.

"She's weird," Brian murmurs as Chester sniffs at the doll.

"I think she was made to be a witch doll." She gives me the shivers, or is it that the temperature has dropped ten degrees in an instant? "Let's rebury this ugly thing quick, before the storm." A streak of lightning signals the urgency, and I drop the doll back in the hole.

Brian squats to the ground and gently lifts her out of her grave. He's such a softy, that brother of mine. "I'm gonna see if she'll fit in one of my baseball-card boxes. Then bury her."

Seems silly to me, but there's no time to argue as the rain makes small plinking dimples in the dirt pile and soon turns into a thunderous torrent that floods the small grave. We dash to the house, kicking our wet shoes off onto the floor of the mudroom. We're soaked to the skin, but Miss Amelia is bone-dry, locked in Brian's hand — which is dripping wet.

Well! That Miss Amelia is a mysterious little doll-person. That's three dolls we've found today, and not one of them seems very playful.

"Gimme the doll, Brian."

He flings his hand behind his back, out of my reach. "You'll toss her in the garbage."

"I will not!" I reply, but it wouldn't be a bad idea. Let her roll around in coffee grounds and bacon grease. "I'm going up to the attic to put her in the dollhouse, which is probably where she came from in the first place."

"Think she's hungry? I'd be."

"You're always hungry. Anyway, you're real. She's not. Face it: Dolls don't eat or drink." Or die and get buried.

Brian looks me squarely in the eye. "She *is* real, Shelby. Maybe I heard her say something."

"Ridiculous!" I huff as I head for the attic. Emily heard things. . . .

I seat Miss Amelia on the bottom step in the front hall of the dollhouse. She topples over onto the floor, her stiff legs letting out a quiet squeal, like they need oiling.

Or is it her voice? So I limber up her legs with a few hearty bends and seat her again on the step, more securely this time. Immediately she falls over again and lands facedown on the fringed Persian rug at the bottom of the staircase. Curious. Twice? It's almost like she's trying to show me something. Patting the floor under her, I feel a bump, maybe a dead bug under there. I peel back the carpeting and — surprise! — there's a small O-ring nailed to the wood, and it's just big enough for me to jam my pinkie into it and give it a pull. A tiny trapdoor pops straight up, revealing a secret compartment under the floor! It's dark inside; I can't see anything, so I reach in and feel around and just miss getting my fingers snapped into a mousetrap. I toss the mousetrap aside (no mouse in it; I'd die on the spot if there were) and probe around in that little hole again until my fingers find a small rectangular thing, which turns out to be a tiny speckled book no larger than a Jolly Rancher candy. Inside are a few blank pages, yellowed with age.

Oh! If this house is an exact copy of our big house, then there must be a secret compartment under the Persian rug at the bottom of our stairs. After Brian and Mom are asleep, I'll explore that space. Who knows what I'll find?

The tiny book's in my jeans pocket, but I close the trapdoor and replace the rug, feeling a little creeped out that I'm being drawn deeper and deeper into the mystery of this house.

As I'm backing down the attic ladder, Mom grabs my arm, and I nearly leap off the ladder.

"You scared me, Mom."

"Your father's on the phone." Mom thrusts the phone into my hand. I don't want to talk to him, but now I hear him saying "Shel?"

"Hello, Dad," I mutter flatly.

"How's the new house?" He's faking so much good cheer that it makes me want to cry. That's one of the weird things about me. I cry when I'm happy, and I cry when I'm angry, but I don't cry when I'm sad. Much.

"House is okay. Lot of old stuff."

"Mom says the kitchen's nice."

He has no right to mention Mom so casually. She doesn't belong to him anymore. And of course neither of us mentions Terri or Marcus, as if we're all pretending that Dad doesn't have a new family he likes better.

"School starts next week, eh?"

"What do you care?"

45

"I do care," he says so quietly that I can hardly hear him. Long pause. We used to be able to talk to each other so easily. Baseball and old Shrek movies and horseback-riding stuff. We had fairy tea parties together when I was still into that girlie stuff a few years ago. When Gram died, Dad was the one who knew just how to break the news to me, but now . . .

"Shelby, honey, I know you're still mad at me."

"I'm not mad!" I holler, snuffing back the tears.

"Angry, angry girl." Did Dad say that? Sounded more like a female voice. Terri better not be on the line!

"Tell her to hang up!" I shout.

"I'm on my cell, Shel. No one else could be listening in."

I hear Marcus in the background asking if he can play with Dad's ivory chess set, the one Dad taught Brian and me on.

"Go play chess, who cares? I have to go." If I don't hang up right now, I'll yell things at Dad that'll feel good now, but will make me feel awful when I play them over and over in my mind later.

Dad sighs. "Okay, honey. Put Brian on, will you?"

I don't care if Dad's still on the line waiting for Brian. I rush outside, letting the screen door slam. Where to?

Maybe I'll jump in that polluted pond with the yellow decayed leaves, roll around in it a few miserable hours, then slog up to my room and bury my dripping head in my pillow. Pond scum on my bed? Ugh.

But next thing I know, I'm kneeling in the muddy grass at the doll graveyard, without a clue about how I got here.

Brian is here, too. And he's already digging.

CHAPTER SEVEN

BRIAN PULLS THE DOLL OUT OF BABY DAISY'S grave and brushes off the wet dirt. She's a fat little thing, maybe two inches tall, with just a little swirling crown of porcelain hair on her perfectly round head. Her cheeks are apple-pink, her mouth a tiny red O, and her ears have dot-sized diamond studs. A fancy white dress falls to her feet, with white stockings folded over, lacy at the ankles. Chester licks her, then, bored, walks away in his princely strut.

"Looks like she's ready for her christening," I tell Brian, looking her over again — the white dress, the lacy socks. Now I notice a blue bow stuck on her ripples of hair, and tiny blue teddy bears on her lacy socks. I'd swear neither of those was there before. Didn't she have light brown hair? Now she's a towhead; her hair's almost white. And a jagged crack zigzags from her left eye to her neck now.

She changes before our eyes! Or our eyes do. There's no explaining it.

Shaken, I manage, "Let's take her up to the dollhouse in the attic so she can be with Miss Amelia." But Brian isn't listening. He's digging again in a frenzy, and up turns Miss Amelia herself.

"How did she get back here?" I ask, shocked. "I put her in the attic a few minutes ago. You reburied her?"

Brian's face is pale, his hands shaky. "Hunh-uh. She got here on her own."

"Impossible!"

"Then, what happened?"

We both start scrambling through the dirt to unearth the next doll, Betsy Anne. I blow the dirt off her flowery dress. Her blond hair is pulled to one side in a braid woven around a magenta ribbon. She's about six inches tall, way too big for the dollhouse in the attic. With such peachy skin and a dainty mouth eternally smiling, she's the prettiest of the dolls we've found so far. I close my eyes for a minute, then look her over carefully to see if anything's changed. "What do you see, Brian?"

"Just a girl in a dress, a pigtail, blue eyes."

"That's what I see," I murmur. "I wonder why Baby Daisy . . ." What's the word? *Morphs* before our eyes.

And then she does it again. This is way too freaky to be normal.

We stash Baby Daisy and Betsy Anne and Miss Amelia down into the dark, damp earth, hoping the worms will find them tasty really soon. Just to be sure, I toss in their three tongue-depressor grave markers, dump dirt over all of it, tamp it down, and stomp the mass grave with my heels. Overkill, yeah, but these are unusual circumstances.

"They're gone," I assure Brian. "Forget about these weirdo dolls."

He looks skeptical. "You think?"

"Let's go up to the attic and get that baby in the bathtub. Maybe she needs to be buried with the others to put them out of our lives." How weird is this that I'm talking about what a porcelain doll *needs*?

The grandfather clock in the second-floor hall bongs five times. Five o'clock already? I glance at the clock in my room. Three thirty. That's more like it.

"Come on, Brian." We trundle up the ladder toward the attic. Chester is trailing us and barking wildly, but he won't go near the dollhouse. I grab Bathtub Baby, who's still facedown in the water, and suddenly notice that there are dolls in every room, lots of them. Brian's words echo in my mind: "Where are the people?" They weren't there before! But here's Betsy Anne in the front parlor, towering over the mantel above the fireplace, and Baby Daisy on all fours, like she's about to crawl across the parlor floor. Miss Amelia is propped up at the window, as if she's looking for someone across the yard. Looking for us?

"This can*not* be!" I cry. "We just buried them!" I scoop the three of them up, tie them into the bottom of my shirt, and climb back down the attic ladder so fast that it's clattering and wobbling. Brian is right behind me, and the dolls are clicking together in the nest of my T-shirt.

Mom's stacking boxes at the bottom of the stairs. "Oh, how nice. You've been up there playing with that charming dollhouse," she says. "Why don't we bring it down to the sunporch?"

Brian and I share a look. Fear shadows across his face. I can only imagine that mine mirrors his. "I don't think so," I tell Mom. "It belongs in the attic."

"All right." Mom waves a beat-up cookbook and says, "I don't want to wait another minute to get into that incredible kitchen. I'm about to make my first trial batch of lentil soup for SerenaStockPot.com. Who wants to be in on this historic moment?"

"Later, Mom," Brian says. "We have to go outside."

"But the ground's soaked." Mom sees me cradling something in the turned-up hem of my shirt. "What are you carrying, Shelby?"

"Oh, just some of the dollhouse people," I calmly reply, but Brian has no sense.

"We buried them out back in the doll cemetery, but somehow they got up here."

Why did he tell her that?! She doesn't know about the doll cemetery, and now she'll ask a million questions, and we'll never get outside, and these dolls rolled in my shirt absolutely will *not* stay still.

Mom just sighs, no questions. She thinks Brian's joking. "Sweetie, isn't that just a tiny bit outrageous?" she says, grinning.

Ooh! If I'd said the dolls magically trounced upstairs on their own, Mom would have a fit and accuse me of lying, which she's been doing a lot since, well, since *it* happened. But Brian just gets the "sweetie" treatment. It is so unfair, just because I'm the oldest.

Mom coaxes Brian. "Come on, sweetie, let's go brew up some soup."

He shakes his head and we hurry outside, determined to get the creepy dolls out of our lives for good. The sky's gray again and seems to turn that way every time we go back to the little cemetery. I kneel in the patch of grave-yard, still fuming at Mom and stabbing the ground with a hand shovel. The dolls tied into my shirt click together some more, almost as if they're chattering, and then I clearly hear a harmony of voices.

The voices must be theirs; there's no one else around.

"Hear that, Brian?" My skin's crawling, because the dolls tied in my shirt are thrumming with life, like I've got a shirt full of crawly worms. Double ugh!

"Hear what?"

He *said* he heard them before. Why not now?

The dolls are still again. "Nothing," I murmur as I dump the three back into the grave and this time cover it with handfuls of rock. Dumb, because pieces of porcelain and stuffing and cloth aren't going to rise up and push the rocks off their graves to get out. I mean, really.

But they did before. Unless Brian dug them up and won't admit it. Or, here's a worse possibility: Are Brian and I totally nuts? Like Emily?

We run back to the house and slam the front door just as the grandfather clock bongs five o'clock again.

CHAPTER EIGHT

"YOU GOTTA KEEP TRACK OF HOW MANY PEOPLE hit your website," Brian says. He's the official techie in the family, but we're all kicking around ideas for SerenaStockPot.com.

"You need a catchy logo, too," I add, scrolling through a bunch of graphics we can adapt for the website.

Mom's making a stack of lists — ingredients, equipment, errands, customers, shipping supplies. "I'd better set up a post office box, oh, and I'll have to buy advertising and figure out how to do online credit-card payments."

"A smartphone will do it, with the right app," Brian says.

Mom groans. "All I really want to do is cook." A diabolical gleam in her eyes tells me there's trouble ahead. "So it's settled, then," she says. "I'll make the soups, freeze-dry them for shipping, and keep the books, and you two will do the computer stuff."

"What? I didn't agree to that!" I shout, at the same time Brian says, "Fair deal, Mom."

"I'll pay," she promises, then adds under her breath, "just as soon as we start to make some money. Next year."

"You have that pile of money from Aunt Amelia," I point out.

"Fifteen thousand dollars doesn't go too far for a start-up business. Besides, we have other bills, and I don't have a job."

"You get money from Dad," I remind her.

Another one of those deep, shuttery sighs: "Yes, but he has two families to support."

The conversation dead-ends, because we're wandering into dangerous territory.

I'm setting up my horrible room, starting with stashing the red velvet bedspread on the floor of the closet. There's a reasonably decent high bureau along one wall, with lots of drawers that I've already filled with underwear and sweaters and tops and jeans and winter hats and mittens. There are still drawers empty. We're shopping for new school clothes this week, though now that Mom says money's a problem, I'm not sure how this is going to work. I *have* to have new clothes for my new school. But then, I guess no one's seen any of my old clothes. A suitcase full of them sits on the closet floor. At least it's a nice, deep closet. I'll take everything out and see what still looks wearable.

Leaning against the back wall of the closet, I feel a strange ribbon of cool air hit my shoulders. Doesn't my closet back up to Brian's next door? So why would cool air be coming from there?

When I knock once and barge into Brian's room, he's deeply concentrating on Mom's laptop. "Just want to check something out in your closet," I explain, and he doesn't even look up. The last rays of sunshine brighten his space. My room's dark, day and night. But I lucked out in the closet department, because his is only about a foot deep. The hangers have to slant sideways to fit, not that he's bothered to hang anything up. Brian's idea of a wardrobe is whatever he wore yesterday. I run my hand along the back wall of the closet, but there's no cool air coming through. Something's odd.

"Find what you were looking for?" Brian asks, eyes still glued to the computer.

"Yeah, sort of."

Back in my room, I check out my closet again. Accounting for its depth, and the skinny closet on other side of the wall, one thing's obvious to me: There's a space between Brian's room and mine! There's no light, and I'm not going downstairs to get the flashlight in the kitchen tool drawer, so I crawl around on the floor and tap the closet wall, looking for a doorknob, a latch, anything that might open up to the space.

There's a hole almost at the floor level. Sticking two fingers into it, I find a latch on the other side and . . . bingo! The wall slides open onto a crawl space just wide enough that my shoulders brush each side. The floor's damp. Roof leaking? That's all we need. I look up and see a small skylight window open about an inch, and there's definitely cool air coming down. And then I spot something round like a drum in the farthest corner. Scooting over, I tap it with my nails. I can hear that it's kind of hollow, but that there's something inside. And there's a yarn thing like a soft handle, so I scoot backward, pulling it with me, until I'm at the opening in the closet wall again.

By the dim light in my room, I see that it's one of those old-fashioned hatboxes, about a foot in diameter. There's an inch of dust on the lid. On the outside, it says *MADAME LOVEAU'S CHAPEAUX FOR THE DISCRIMINATING WOMAN.* Under that it says *Paris World's Fair, 1925.* I shake the box, and something clunks around inside, something too heavy to be a hat. It's delicious to guess what's in the box before I open it: a velvet drawstring sack full of gold coins, maybe. A fur collar like Gram used to wear. Chinese silk slippers. A gold mesh blouse with a hundred buttons down the back.

Or it could be a bunch of dead roaches or dried-up peanut-butter-and-jelly sandwiches crawling with ants. I'm afraid to open it — I'll be grossed out or disappointed. I don't know which is worse. Oh, well. I start to lift the lid when Mom knocks at my door and doesn't wait for me to say "Come in."

"What's that you've got, Shelby? I don't remember that hatbox."

"I found it in the closet."

"What's inside?" Mom asks, her face bright with excitement.

Slowly, I lift the lid and unfold a doll the size of a real baby, but it's an adult-type doll in a flowing gown with layers of silk and gauzy material, eyelet lace, tiny gems, and ribbons, all of it in lots of golden shades. Brocade high-heeled slippers poke out under the long gown. Her hair is the color of Ariel's, the Disney mermaid, and her skin is light enough to practically see through, except for the circles of rouge painted on her cheeks.

"She's beautiful," Mom says, a catch in her throat. "Quite the elegant lady."

My mind switches to that larger grave set apart from the circle of graves, and the marker: *Lady R.I.P.* Not another doll that escaped from the grave! But there's something nagging at my memory. I rummage around in a box of junk I haven't found a place for yet, tossing out useless things I just can't part with. Sheltered under a mangy stuffed pig is a wrinkled mess of lacy gold fabric and ribbons.

"Look, Mom, her hat. It matches her dress!" I smooth the hat out on the doll's cherry-red hair, tying it under her chin. It flops around her delicate porcelain face, as if it's shading her from the sun.

I know who she is. She's Isabella, the one Aunt Amelia told me about, the one with "friends in high places." So why is there no grave for her? Or are Isabella and Lady the same doll? Now I'm curious about the dolls we haven't dug up yet, but also scared to find them.

Mom picks Isabella up and straightens the folds of the gown to smooth out the wrinkles. "Let's set her up on your bureau," Mom says, propping the doll against the mirror. "What a wonderful find. See? I told you good things would happen here. Now, why did I come upstairs? Oh, well, I'll think of it later. I've got three pots on the stove, so I'd better get back to my heavenly kitchen."

I can't take my eyes off the doll facing me, her back reflected in the mirror. She is beautiful, but her pale face looks vacant, her eyes staring into thin air, as though life has been somehow sucked out of her and left her a sad doll. Paris, 1925. This doll is really old and probably valuable. Maybe we could sell her, if Mom needs money. But why was she hidden away in the closet? Was it to protect her, to keep her out of the grave? Or to protect someone from her?

Emily? No, the thick dust on the lid tells me that Emily never handled this doll. For some reason she was hidden so well that she'd never, ever be found. Was this Sadie's doing?

Isabella blinks. Did I just imagine that? She blinks again, and suddenly I think I know why she's been hidden away for so long.

Because she must have scared the living daylights out of Sadie Thornewood nearly eighty years ago!

CHAPTER NINE

IT'S ALMOST EIGHT O'CLOCK AND GETTING DARK, but Mom's still going strong in the kitchen, humming and singing Broadway show tunes. She hasn't been this happy since, well, *he* left. I wish she'd finish up, though, because I want to see what's under the floor at the foot of our stairs. But I'm dog-tired, and so is Chester, the actual dog — the two of us could just drift off to sleep right here on the steps. My eyes snap open and drift shut and snap open. . . .

Nine forty-five, and the lights are still on in the kitchen. "It's hopeless, Chester. We might as well go to bed." I drag myself up to my room and flop down on my spindly bed with the mattress that's about two inches thick and feels like it's stuffed with prickly hay. I'll bet a cot jutting out from the wall in a jail cell is more comfy. Chester doesn't even bother hopping up on the bed. So I lie there on my back, looking around and trying to figure out how to turn the room into a space I'd actually want to wake up in. Isabella — or is she Lady? — still sits on my bureau, her golden gown billowing out around her. Those vacant eyes are making me feel squirmy, so I turn to face the wall, but it feels like someone's watching me. A quick peek at her under my arm startles me, and I bolt up in bed, sending the bed springs squawking like mad. Her eyes are definitely different now. She *is* watching me! I jump up, scaring Chester, who's sleeping on the rug next to my bed, and I turn Isabella so her back's to me.

That's worse, because now I see her face in the mirror, and that'll be even spookier in the middle of the night. Up again, this time shoving her into one of the empty drawers, which I slam shut. Then I pull my pillow down to the floor and curl up around Chester.

In the morning a little light leaks into my cave. I'm shivering because I never dragged a blanket down to the floor last night, and Chester's warmth isn't enough on this cold morning. I nervously look over at the bureau and the drawer where I tucked Isabella away. It's wide open! Some of her gown hangs over the drawer, and her tall, laced boots have fallen off onto the floor. This is not possible!

There's got to be a logical explanation. Sure. Mom must have come upstairs to tuck me in like she used to before *he* left, and when she didn't see Isabella on the bureau, she poked around until she found her and just never closed the drawer. Simple.

But I feel in my bones, that's not what happened.

I pick Isabella up. She's more solid than I remembered, and warm, the kind of warm you are first thing in the morning, all cozy under the covers — if you don't fall asleep on the floor. Her arms and legs don't bend easily, and I get the eerie idea that she's deliberately resisting my movements. Our eyes lock. Hers are brown-green, what Gram called hazel, like mine. We're playing chicken; which one will blink first? I'm good at this. Brian and I do it all the time, and I can go for a full minute without blinking. But this is stupid; she's a *doll*. I'm alive, and she's not, so I let my eyes flutter madly, just to show her I can.

Her cherry curls are soft, not wiry like you'd expect on a doll. I take her huge satin-and-lace hat off to check out her glued-on wig, but I'm amazed to see that the doll maker has planted each hair in her scalp separately. Human hair. If that's not creepy, I don't know what is. What girl's head did it come from? Was she dead when her hair was plucked off, one curly hair at a time?

She blinks! She's mocking me, making fun of me, and I hear — no, *imagine* — her saying, "Shelby Tate is an ignoramus. I, myself, am a refined lady of the court of St. James, and she is but a country bumpkin. Ha!"

Okay, she asked for it! I stuff her and her billowing gown and ridiculous floppy hat and wild hair into the one drawer in my bureau that has a key sticking out of it. With lots of pleasure, I lock her in and drop the key into my sock, where no one will find it to let her out. Ha, yourself, Isabella, or Lady, or whoever you really are!

I'm nervously pacing the floor at the bottom of the stairs, dying to get into what's under there — tonight, for sure — when I hear wheels crunching the gravel outside. I throw the door open to see who could possibly be coming to visit us, and there's a Yellow Cab pulling into our driveway. My first thought is, *Dad's here!* But of course that makes no sense, because he lives two hundred miles away, and even if he were here, he wouldn't come by taxi. Besides, he's a lot more athletic than the old man whose right leg slowly emerges from the taxi, joined even more slowly by his left leg, with a crooked walking stick between them, and then there's a sort of rocking motion to propel the man to his feet. He stands up, spreads his arms like an eagle with the cane pointing skyward, and announces in a booming voice, "I have arrived. Let the show begin."

"That would be Mr. Caliberti," Mom says, wiping her hands on her apron. "Remember? Aunt Amelia told us that he now owns her cottage out back. I believe she said Canto Caliberti is his stage name."

The taxi driver begins unloading boxes and suitcases, including some tied to the roof, until Mr. Caliberti is surrounded by it all.

"My worldly possessions." He squints in our direction. "Ah, you must be the illustrious Tate family. Dear departed Amelia did not tell me there were two sisters."

Mom snickers and says, "I'm Serena, and this is my daughter, Shelby. Welcome home."

"How entirely curious, at this stage of my vagabond life, that I should become a property owner. Well, let us away to my cottage in the countryside, ladies," and he motions for us to begin carrying his worldly possessions.

At the cottage door, he pulls a key on a string out from under his shirt and leans into the door. This is our first peek into Aunt Amelia's cottage in ages. It's neat and plain, like her, with hand-crocheted afghans tossed over the backs of the couch and easy chair, and three towers of books, floor to ceiling, along one wall. A small round kitchen table sits in a little arched alcove, with one chair tidily tucked under it. But what really surprises me — and Mom, too, I'll bet — is that there are pictures of Mom and Brian and me everywhere, even one of the four of us, *before*.

"Just set things down pell-mell, ladies, pell-mell, while I have a look around." He stands in the center of the living room and slowly revolves. "Ah, she is everywhere," he says.

Mom asks, "Would you like to have dinner with us this evening, Mr. Caliberti, since you're not yet settled?"

"Kind of you, but I must decline. Best to establish my routine here from Act One, Scene One." He flips on the porch light, even though it's a brisk, sunny day. "I trust the light will not disturb you? There are so many superstitions in the theater." He pronounces it "THEE-uh-tah," with a flair. "One of them is the necessity of the ghost light."

My ears perk up. "What's a ghost light, Mr. Caliberti?"

"Oh, child, have you no THEE-uh-tah experience? We shall have to change that. The ghost light burns day and night outside the stage door, to keep the ghosts within at bay. Now, I must ask you to bring the rest of my worldly possessions in posthaste, as I'm dragging a bit after an all-night flight from Kathmandu."

Mom yells for Brian to help, and we get everything into the cottage quickly, just as Mr. Caliberti is releasing his cat from a mesh travel bag. He kisses the cat on the nose and says, "Terpsichore, meet the Tate family. Amelia's people."

CHAPTER TEN

MIDNIGHT. THE HOUSE IS DARK EXCEPT FOR A DIM light over the stove, barely visible out here in the entrance hall. By flashlight I roll up the rug to expose the floor, and there it is, a small thumbhole like in my closet wall, with the latch inside. The trapdoor squeals as I lift it. While I'm waiting a minute to make sure the noise hasn't awakened anyone, I wonder how many other secret compartments were built into this house so long ago and whether Sadie knew about all of them. What about Emily? Are there clues and secrets locked away all over this house that other girls who lived here found, clues that reveal the mystery of the dolls?

Lying on my stomach, I shine the flashlight into the hole under the floor, to make sure there are no booby traps or mousetraps to scare me off. The hole seems to be about a foot deep and maybe two feet wide, curiously lined with soft wool carpeting. Now, why would the builder bother to carpet a secret compartment? Or did Sadie do it, to provide a cozy place for her dolls to live? Under the floor? How weird is that?

It's there, smack in the middle of the compartment, exactly what I knew I'd find — a notebook like the one in the dollhouse, but lots bigger. Just as I reach for it, someone pushes me from behind. Brian! He jams my head down into the wool carpet and slams the trapdoor against my back. I'm stuck half in, half out of that secret compartment. I can't believe my brother would do this to me, but I can't yell and wake Mom. With my arms flailing around behind me, I manage to shove the trapdoor up and pull my head out. I *will* make Brian pay for this.

"Brian Tate," I growl. "Where are you, you little snot?"

On my feet now, I swing the flashlight all over, looking for a foot sticking out from underneath a couch, or something knocked over in his hurry to hide. I expect to see him crawl out, shielding his eyes against the bright light, with a smug smile on his freckled face.

But there's no sign of Brian.

I tiptoe upstairs, creep into his room. He's sprawled out on his back, one foot sticking out of the covers, the way he usually sleeps. I whisper his name. Louder. If he's faking sleep, he's doing a real good job of it. When I shake his shoulder there's a whiny "Whaddya want?"

"You were downstairs a minute ago, right? Tried to shove me into the space under the floor?"

He blinks, clearing sleep out of his eyes. "Huh?"

"Tell the truth, Brian Tate!"

His face looks totally innocent in the shadowy green glow of his Yoda night-light. Even Brian isn't that good an actor, and then I know, as sure as I know my own heartbeat, that it wasn't Brian who pushed me.

But then, who was it?

"Go back to sleep," I tell him, and I head for my own room.

The dolls. I'm beginning to think those dolls, from tiny Baby Daisy to Isabella herself, are possessed or magical or ghostly or evil or something I don't have a word for, and that they haunt this house.

No, they rule it.

But I'll show *them*! I've got the notebook.

Huddling under a tent of blankets, I shine my flashlight on the notebook. It's one of those old speckled composition books. Taking a deep breath, I open it to page one, which is blank. So is page two. In fact, flipping through the notebook, I'm crushed to see that the whole thing is blank. I went through so much to snag this, and now it's going to tell me absolutely nothing? So not fair! I run an index finger over a random page as if something were actually written there that I could read in Braille, not that I read Braille.

Strange, I do feel little bumps in the paper, but not Braille dots, exactly. Page after page has the same slightly bumpy feel, as though something were once written there but erased.

Or written in invisible ink!

How do you read invisible ink? Clutching the notebook, I quietly creep downstairs to the dining room to wake up Mom's laptop. All I have to do is key in *read invisible ink*, and it's simple: Heat will show the words. I could hold a page over a stove burner, but what if it caught fire? Ugh. I hate fire. I glance up at the smoke alarm over the stove. That would wake the whole house, even the dolls. Then I get a totally brilliant idea. There's a fold-down ironing board in the laundry-room wall. I turn on the iron, making sure there's no water, because steam would ruin the paper and I'd never see what's written on it. It'll work, I'm sure. I'll just put page one facedown on the board and run a warm iron over the back of the page and — huh! It's coming clear, scratched out in a child's uphill-slanted handwriting:

The Incredible True Adventures of Me
by Sadie Isabella Thornewood
Read it, and you will have bad luck just like me
forever and ever!

That warning won't stop me. I'm way too curious, so I'll risk it. Wait, that little hat Aunt Amelia gave me. She said it was for a doll named Isabella, and when I found her and tried the hat on her, it fit perfectly. It's no coincidence, I'm sure, that the doll and Sadie Thornewood share a name. I guess this is one of the loose ends Aunt Amelia warned me about.

This is going to be a slow, boring process, ironing each page, and I lose words that are too close to the binding, so I have to guess at what's missing at the beginning or end of the lines. My heart sinking, I realize it's not as easy as I thought it would be to piece it all together:

... almost finished digging the graveyard when

...Baby Daisy can't see anything now 'cause I colored over her eyes with India ink and scratched out her

...wiped it off cuz she was so mad at me and made me eat dirt which

I flip to a random page in the middle of the notebook, and the word that seems to pop out at me is *Lady*. Does it mean anything that *Sadie* and *Lady* rhyme? A little more heat, and I read, *I hate, hate, hate her!!!* That seems really important, but as hard as I slam the iron back and forth over the page, nothing else shows up. The page is truly blank. Was Sadie just too spooked to write anything more about Lady? Is Lady really Isabella, the one from the hatbox? Sure, she creeped me out last night, but is that enough to *hate* her with such venom that Sadie repeated the word three times? I mean, she's just a doll. Isn't she?

There's got to be a better, quicker way to read this stuff. Back to the laptop. The famous lightbulb goes off over my head, because that's the solution. If I hold a page under a lightbulb, the words will magically appear. Mom's got one of those high-intensity lamps on her desk, and as the paper warms in my hands, I make out five words that chill me to the bone:

. . . I'm so, so, so scared!!!

And then the page goes blank again, and besides, I've held the paper so close to the lamp that it's burned a little hole in it.

So I scroll through a bunch of website info about invisible ink until I find the best solution: ultraviolet light. That's like the goggles you see in movies that crooks use to see in pitch-dark. But I'm sure there's nothing like that in Mom's kitchen tool drawer. And now it's after midnight, and I need to get to sleep. Tomorrow I'll figure out how to get an ultraviolet penlight. I'll think of something. Maybe if I concentrate hard enough, I'll dream a way to do it.

CHAPTER ELEVEN

At breakfast, Mom says, "Well, Shelby, I see you've been ironing! Or was it you, Brian?"

"Hunh-uh."

Mom turns back to me. "Excellent. I'll turn all the family ironing over to you from now on."

I nearly spit out a mouthful of oatmeal. Why didn't I fold up the ironing board? She'd never have known. Family ironing drudgery is not what I had in mind. But then the imaginary lightbulb flashes over my head again with my second and most brilliant idea. If Mom wants me to iron, and I want an ultraviolet penlight, maybe we can work out a business arrangement. I'll iron a few blouses, and she'll buy me the ten-dollar UV pen I saw online. Good deal!

I float the idea. "You know, what I really need is an ultraviolet penlight."

"What on earth would you need such a thing for?" Mom asks.

Think fast! "Brian and I are doing this secret-code experiment."

"We are?"

Well, it's almost true, but now I'm going to have to let Brian in on it, or I'll never get the pen.

Mom's face lights up. "So glad you're playing with your brother. That makes me think our little family's returning to some sort of normal again."

Normal isn't your father living with some *other family*. Normal isn't dolls that refuse to stay buried, or who turn up in odd places, or who change before your eyes, or whose eyes stare you down. Normal isn't someone pushing you into a hole in the floor. If she only knew. "Yes, things are much better," I say, though I feel a little guilty keeping all this from Mom.

"All right, sweetie, show me the website, and I'll order the light." A few clicks and it's mine! But, how disappointing. It'll take five business days to get here. Phew. That means I'll already be in school, and I suppose I have to start acting like I'm playing with Brian, who's right now looking at me with a happy puppy-dog expression that says, *Whaddya want to do? Pitch me soft-balls? Play chess? Trade* Star Wars *cards?*

None of the above. "Hey, Brian, let's go see if there's any fish in that pond out back."

"All right!"

I don't mention that we have no fishing rods and that I'm not at all interested in the pond. But I do want to go explore that doll graveyard again, especially the grave marked *Lady.* I just don't want Mom to know about it yet.

She's beyond thrilled. "Oh, you two are so adorable together. Leave the ironing until later, Shelby. Go on out to the pond. It might be the last nice day of summer before school starts next Tuesday. Go play. Go be kids. Happy kids."

We bolt out the door so fast that the windows in the kitchen shudder.

"Forget the stinky old pond, Brian. Let's go to the doll graveyard."

He looks a little panicky and says, "Okay, I guess."

Someone's already beat us to the clearing where the graves are. The old man, Mr. Caliberti, is sitting on one of those little stools that double as a cane. He doesn't hear us coming, because he's talking to himself. It must be to himself, since there's no one else around. Unless he's having a chat with the dead dolls.

"Shh, let's not scare him," I whisper to Brian.

Mr. Caliberti's back snaps up. He must have seen our shadows. "Well, don't just stand there in the wings. Come around stage left," he says in a snippy voice.

"It's just us, Brian and Shelby."

"Yes, and you've found me. I've come to visit old friends."

Mr. Caliberti's cat, Terpsichore — isn't that a dumb name for a cat? — darts out of some nearby bushes and arches her back at the sight of us. She leaps onto Mr. C's lap, her yellow eyes glaring at me as if she thinks I'm try-ing to take her master away from her. I mean, really, she can have the cranky old man.

Brian plops down on the ground, and Mr. Caliberti snarls, "Not there, young Mr. Brian. That spot's reserved for Dotty, can't you see?"

One of the grave markers that we buried so deep is jutting out of the ground again.

Scurrying to his feet, Brian mumbles, "Sor-ree."

"She was a delightful character, Dorothy Grabowski was, cute as a button, but couldn't hold a candle to my sweetheart, my leading lady."

Now I'm totally confused. Are we talking about a doll, or a person?

"Came out west here from Iowa, I believe, to be young Sadie's governess."

He knew Sadie!

"Who's Sadie?" asks Brian.

"Why, she was the older of the two sisters, one sweet as summer corn, that would be Baby Daisy. The other was sharp as horseradish."

Brian looks over at the grave marked *Baby Daisy*. Like me, he must be thinking about how we buried and reburied her, and still she somehow got up to the attic and found her way to the dollhouse.

"Yes, Dorothy was a joy, full of laughter. But Sadie despised her, along with just about everybody else on God's magnificent stage. Well, I must admit, Dorothy did have some rather unconventional notions."

"Like what, Mr. Caliberti?" asks Brian.

"Ever pick dandelions?"

"He loves me, he loves me not," I murmur, plucking and tossing imaginary leaves. Even though there's no wildflower in my hand, I can smell the slightly salty-bitter scent of a dandelion.

"Ever eat them?"

"Eww, no way," Brian cries.

"Well, now, Dorothy sprinkled crumbled dandelions over everything those three girls put to their mouths, including the baby. Dorothy believed that dandelions were rich in vitamins and wholesome minerals, and that's why she had such a peachy complexion. She did, too. Pure Iowa farm-girl skin.

"Now, Sadie, she thought Dorothy Grabowski was a lunatic, especially when the young woman howled during the full-moon nights. So, Sadie nicknamed her Dotty Woman. You young people still use the word *dotty*? It means 'not right in the head.'"

Like Emily. "I want to hear more about Sadie," I tell him quietly.

"You do, do you? You wouldn't if you knew her the way I knew her. She was one mean-tempered, foot-stamping, jealous vixen, as spoiled as Tuesday's fish."

"Wow!" Brian says. "She sounds like a real winner."

Mr. Caliberti is lost in his own memories now. "Jealous of everyone and everything, but mostly of my sweetheart, who was the daughter of the Thornewoods' housekeeper, Celeste. They lived in. We were but children ourselves, then, I twelve, she nine. My father was the groundskeeper." He glances around. "Those days, it was quite a luscious spread, not gone to seed the way it is now." He closes one eye and inspects Brian. "About your size, my sweetheart was when I met her. I was besotted by her from the first day. I've loved her all my life long. Unfortunately, I was in Xanadu at the time of her recent passing and wasn't able to attend the service."

Xanadu? I was sure he'd said Kathmandu the day we met him. Oh, well, it's all very swoony romantic, but what I really want to hear about is Sadie. "Mr. Caliberti, did Sadie have a lot of dolls?"

"Why do you ask?" he says sharply. "Sadie Thornewood had a lot of everything, except good manners. Mr. Thornewood indulged her, brought her the finest costumes from Paris, soft leather boots from Italy, and an entire collection of antique porcelain dolls, life-size German-made ones and small ones no bigger than Tom Thumb."

"She must have loved those dolls," I murmur, fishing for more information.

Mr. Caliberti wrinkles up his brow and pushes off from the seat by leaning on the cane handle. Terpsichore goes flying. "Loved them? Nonsense. She yelled at those innocent playthings and tossed them about and called them vile names. Once I had to stay her hand to keep her from smashing one with my father's garden shears."

He's a little wobbly on his feet. He tests the ground with his folded-up cane seat and whistles for Terpsichore, who leads him out of the little clearing. Before he's gone too far, he calls to us over his shoulder — from offstage, as Mr. Caliberti might say.

"Young Mr. Brian, young Miss Shelby, you missed your cue. You did not ask the name of my sweetheart. Amelia, she was. Dear departed Amelia." And he walks away, his shoulders rounded forlornly.

CHAPTER TWELVE

"MOM, DID YOU KNOW THAT AUNT AMELIA AND Mr. Caliberti had a *thing* going?"

"What sort of thing, Shelby?" Mom asks, ladling minestrone soup into our bowls. I'm hungry for something besides soup, soup, soup, like a nice juicy hamburger and McDonald's fries.

"She was his girlfriend," Brian says. "That old lady and old man? Gross."

Mom pauses, ladle in midair dripping pinkish juices. "She never talked about a gentleman in her life, and she never married."

I break a saltine in the soup and watch the crumbs bloat in the liquid. Maybe I should tell Mom about the dolls.

Slurping fills the silence. "Stop sucking the soup off your spoon, Brian. Manners."

And that reminds me of Mr. Caliberti saying that Sadie had everything except good manners. If there's anyone like Sadie Thornewood at my new school, I'll make sure I sit clear across the room. No, I'm not ready to tell Mom about the dolls yet. I need to do a little more investigating.

"Of course, Aunt Amelia did leave the cottage to Mr. Caliberti. I wondered about that," Mom says. "Ice-cream sandwiches for dessert when you finish your soup."

I keep swallowing spoonfuls, and the level never goes down in my bowl. Why couldn't SerenaStockPot .com have been SerenasPizza.com or SerenasOodles-of-Noodles.com?

Brian tells us, "Mr. Caliberti uses funny words, like from a different planet."

Mom smiles and lays her spoon in the saucer under the bowl. "Are you as sick of soup as I am?"

We both drop our spoons; Brian's lands on the floor, so Chester gets a good lick of it.

"Let's order a pizza," Mom suggests.

Yes!

Just before dinner Brian and I had climbed up to the attic with two flashlights to bring everything in the doll-house to light. All the people were gone again, so I guess they stayed buried this time. Sadie's little house looked so deserted. Lucky girl; her father loved her so much that he had that house built for her. So how did it end up abandoned in the attic?

On Saint Patrick's Day when I was nine, Dad made me a hinged box with ten little compartments for all my barrettes and earrings. It was such a cool box with a cute little winking leprechaun on the lid, sitting in a field of four-leaf clover. There was a card with it, signed, *You're my good-luck charm, Shelby. Love always, Daddy.*

I left it in the old house.

Just thinking about it now makes me mad. I can feel the heat of my anger creeping up my spine.

"Half pepperoni, half black olive," Mom's saying into the phone. "Yes, it's that little clump of houses called Cinder Creek." Pause. "It's not the end of the earth. Look it up on your GPS, for heaven's sake."

She's mad like I am, though only about some stupid pizza-delivery guy who doesn't feel like driving all the way out here. Dad left her, too. He left all of us. But I'm the only one who still seems to care. Mom slams down the phone with a huff, and then I hear a voice that isn't hers or Brian's:

"Angry, angry girl." Now it's a chorus of voices, all out of sync, like when you sing "Row, Row, Row Your Boat" in three parts. Mom checks her wallet; she hasn't heard the voices, and Brian's clueless, just finger-painting the table with minestrone.

"MOM!" I shout.

Startled, she spins around.

"I have to tell you something."

And so I pour it all out, but it's a seesaw — me up high with relief, and Mom sinking low with worry. She gets that very calm drawl that she uses when she's in the middle of some kind of disaster. It's the voice she used the night she and Dad told us they were splitting up.

"All right, these dolls . . . I know you found that one in the hatbox that was left in your closet by a previous tenant."

"Deliberately hidden in a secret compartment in my closet and not supposed to be found." Except that Aunt Amelia *wanted* me to find Isabella. Did she remember the hiding place from eighty years back?

"I can't imagine why she'd be hidden. She's lovely."

"Her eyes follow me," I tell Mom flatly, and she replies, "Uh-huh," which means "I don't believe you."

"Shelby, honey, let me see if I have this straight: These assorted dolls are in and around our house."

"There's a graveyard of 'em," Brian adds. "Only they don't stay dead."

Mom's head whips around to Brian. "You've seen these dolls coming and going, too?"

The voices are still there. It's hard to concentrate with them streaming through my head, but I try to explain: "We don't actually see them coming and going. We just see them when they end up where we didn't put them."

All of a sudden Brian bursts into a zillion words. "I told you the other day, Mom. You didn't believe me. We buried them, and they got unburied and went upstairs to the dollhouse, and they tried to drown the baby in the bathtub and Shelby and me buried 'em again and put rocks over their graves, and one of 'em's named Miss Amelia." Brian sinks back in his chair, proud to prove his point.

"Let's get this clear," Mom says calmly. "Brian, we both know that you have a way of following your sister wherever she leads you."

"Gimme a break, Mom!"

"You have to admit all this is a little hard to swallow." Turning to me, she says, "Shelby, we also know that you tend to be a bit of a drama queen, exaggerating things, embellishing now and then. You've always had an active fantasy life. All those castles and princesses and fairies and goblins you used to read about."

And leprechauns. "This is different. This is real."

Mom closes her eyes and takes a deep breath. "Could it be possible, honey, that you need to talk to someone?"

"I'm talking to you, and you don't believe me!"

"I mean, talk to someone professionally."

"What profession?" I ask.

"A psychologist. A good child psychologist. There must be someone in Trinidad."

"You think I'm crazy?"

"No! Just a little carried away. I know it's been difficult with your father gone and all. Oh, I thought moving out of Denver would be the new start we all needed."

I'm still hearing "Angry girl, tsk tsk, such an angry girl, isn't she, Dotty?" "Oh, indeed, look how red her face is. Why, Betsy Anne, I do believe she might burst like a bag of confetti."

They're discussing me, like I'm not even in the room. Maybe I am crazy, same as Emily. Or maybe Emily wasn't crazy at all.

The pizza arrives, but Brian and Chester are the only ones who eat it.

CHAPTER THIRTEEN

WHEN THE PHONE RINGS, THAT OLD KIND OF wailing ring, we all jump. It's been a long time since we've had a landline like this house has. I pick up the clunky black receiver upstairs just as Mom gets the kitchen phone. It's Dad.

"Why didn't you call on my cell, Sam?"

"That's a real warm greeting."

Already they're off and running.

"Doesn't matter," Mom says. "I was going to call you later today anyway. I'm worried about Shelby."

Oh no! Why does she have to drag him into this?

"What's going on with her that isn't going on with every other preteen girl?"

Dad's trying to joke around, but Mom's having none of it. I can tell by the irritation in her voice. "She's obsessed with some dolls previous occupants left here. She claims they're talking to her."

"Like her teddy bear Trombone and that four-foot giraffe did when she was little?"

"As usual, Sam, you're missing the point. With the animals, she knew it was imaginary. Now she believes they really are talking to her, and moving around on their own, and she's got Brian believing it, too. Shelby has buried these dolls in a little graveyard on the property, which is bizarre in itself, but she says they're getting out of the graves and going where they please. You see? It sounds insane."

"What's Brian say about all this?" Dad asks.

"He says the same thing, but you know how he's always followed her lead, and besides, there's that bout of lying we went through right after."

There's no need to say "After what?"

Back and forth they go, she asking why he hasn't come to see us, as the court ordered, and he accusing her of making it impossible by taking us nearly two hundred miles away from him. I tune out, until she says, "Shelby needs new clothes. School starts next week."

"Tomorrow, Terri and I will drive down and take her shopping."

Not with Terri!

Mom saves me: "No, Sam. Alone."

"All right. What's the nearest shopping mall to you?"

"Google it," Mom snaps.

I press the phone against my shoulder. My head's throbbing with anger at both of them, and I've had enough. I don't want to hear what he barks back at her. What I hear instead is, "Calm your rage, angry girl. Take a deep breath."

Is it my conscience talking to me? With the phone pressed to me, Dad's voice vibrates through my body. Yes, I must have imagined it because I'm still flustered over the thought of shopping with Terri.

When it seems safe to listen again, I raise the phone back to my ear.

"All right, Serena, you win. I'll pick her up about noon Saturday. We'll have a few hours, and then I'll come get Brian. I'll get a hotel room somewhere. He can spend the night with me."

"That'll work," Mom says.

Well, it won't work for me. But before I can tell them that, I hear a distinct voice unlike the ones I've heard before. It's an elegant, princesslike voice, a little bit British. Could it be Lady?

"Why, oh, why is it only the angriest, nastiest-tempered

girls who abide within our walls? I, for one, am weary of it. The time has come for us to do something, would you all agree?"

There's a resounding, echoey chorus: "Indeed. Revenge!"

❈ ◉ ❈

Now more than ever, I need to know what's in Sadie's notebook, because I'm scared of what the dolls have in mind. Holding pages up under a lightbulb is slow and painful, and I keep burning my fingers on the lightbulb and sucking them to cool them. The penlight hasn't landed in our mailbox yet.

I've let Brian in on the whole notebook thing, but I made him promise not to say a word to Mom yet. "And that goes for Dad, too," I warn. "You're spending Saturday night with him at a hotel. Don't say one single word about this diary."

"Saturday night, really? Will the hotel have a pool? Should I take my Spidey trunks? My mitt and bat?"

"I don't know," I answer impatiently. I've got my own worries about what I'm going to say to Dad all those hours on Saturday afternoon. "Stop jiggling the flashlight.

Hold it steady, right there." We're on the floor in my room, trying to decipher Sadie's words, but the flashlight isn't hot enough.

The desk lamp! It takes a while for the paper to heat enough to give up a few words.

Brian's very impressed. "It's like spies. Like a secret code, only you don't have to say every *A* equals *Z* and stuff like that." He's going on and on about variations of secret codes when the words start to appear:

. . . brought them from his last business trip to Germany, or maybe some other European . . .

. . . if only my head didn't hurt so much, I could . . .

. . . picked the ugliest one to be Amelia 'cause I hate . . .

. . . said he'd bring me a chartreuse parrot from the Amazon rain forest next . . .

. . . Mother loves Daisy lots more. She's always hugging . . .

. . . Amelia's mother gave her three . . .

"This doesn't make any sense, Shelby."

"I think it might." I try piecing all this together to

come up with a reasonable story. "Sadie was a real unhappy girl."

"Mean, Mr. Caliberti said."

"Yes, but why? People aren't born mean. Things happen to turn them that way. Here's what I'm thinking: Sadie was a little spoiled because her father gave her everything she wanted. I mean, a parrot from the Amazon rain forest? Come on. He even built that dollhouse for her that's a perfect model of our house, down to the smallest details. But look, it says he took lots of business trips. Maybe she felt neglected. Maybe he gave her stuff to make up for not being around."

"Dad's not around," Brian says quietly, "and he's not sending us stuff."

Brian's words break my heart, so I quickly say, "Yes, but Dad knows that Mom's looking after us. Sadie says right here that her mother loves Daisy, her little sister, and not Sadie. So who's taking care of Sadie Thornewood?"

"A maid or something?" Brian asks.

"She's called a nanny, or a governess. Remember, Mr. Caliberti said that Dotty Woman, the dandelion lady, was the governess for those two sisters. The housekeeper was Amelia's mother. That's our Aunt Amelia when she was a little girl. She and Gram and their mother the housekeeper lived here in this house."

"Aunt Amelia was never a little girl," Brian says.

"Sure she was! Gram was a little girl once. Even Mom and Dad were kids a long time ago. We don't know much about Dotty Woman, only that Mr. Caliberti said she laughed a lot, and Sadie thought she was nuts." There seems to be a lot of that going around in this house. "But let's say Amelia's mother loved Daisy more than she loved Sadie, and of course she loved her own daughter even more. Sadie had to be feeling totally unloved."

Brian's lost interest in the conversation and is much more fascinated by the hole that's burning in the paper, which I snatch away from him. Returning to Sadie's handwriting, I zero in on a line:

...picked the ugliest one to be Amelia 'cause I hate...

What if Sadie took those dolls her father brought her from Europe, and she pretended that each one was a person who lived in the house? And then she treated them awful, even tried to smash one with garden shears, like Mr. Caliberti said.

Because she was an angry, angry girl. Like me.

I slam the notebook shut and flick off the lamp. "Get lost," I growl at my poor, sweet brother.

CHAPTER FOURTEEN

IT'S SO COLD. IN THE MIDDLE OF THE NIGHT I GOT up and put on a sweatshirt hoodie and some long PJ pants that I hardly ever wear, and now that the sun's coming up, it's even worse. It's only September second. It shouldn't be this cold already.

Downstairs, Mom's wearing a hoodie and a coat and already has three pots of soup simmering on the stove.

"Why's it so cold in here, Mom?"

"Furnace went out. I have to call a heating guy this morning. It better be something he can fix easily, because we can't afford a new one." Warming her hands over one of the steamy pots, she says in a fake-cheerful voice, "There's nothing like a nice, thick split-pea soup to warm the belly. Or tomato bisque or mushroom barley, whichever you prefer."

"Just some toast," I mutter, opening a giant jar of chunky peanut butter.

"When the soup's ready, why don't you take a quart to that nice neighbor, Mariah? It's bound to be tastier than that muscle-bound beefsteak-and-kidney pie."

I can see my breath. "How soon can we get the heat repairman here?"

"Probably not today, but I'll call. Come warm your hands over here."

The three soup smells don't blend into anything you'd really want to sink a spoon into, but the heat rising off a simmering pot feels good. Then suddenly, all three come to a rolling boil, with giant bubbles rising to the top like hot sea foam. We have to jump aside to keep from being scalded as all three pots spill over at once, spewing green, red, and brown soup everywhere.

"That shouldn't have happened," Mom says, along with a dirty word. "Oh no, and now all that spilled soup has drowned out the pilot light." She gives me a roll of paper towels and a pail of soapy water for cleanup, muttering, "What a rotten way to start the day."

It's got to get better fast, because Dad will be here by lunchtime, and that's plenty of drama for one day.

I'm sticky with soup to my elbows, so once I'm done mopping up, I dash upstairs for a hot shower to take the chill out of my bones, and that's when I discover my favorite red sweater crumpled in a wet mess on the floor, cradling a batch of Brian's *Star Wars* figures. Luke Skywalker's lightsaber has snagged the knit, and it's got an ugly loopy hole in it. I was going to wear it on the first day of school, and now it's totally ruined.

"BRIAN!" I scream, whirling into his bedroom like a tornado. "I hate you!"

He's not in his room. I hear footsteps overhead. There's nothing up there but the attic and the dollhouse. What's Brian doing up there, unless he's hiding from me because he knows I'm fuming with steam coming out of both ears.

I scuttle up the pull-down ladder to the attic, ready to wring his skinny chicken neck like in that Jerry Spinelli book *Wringer.* "How could you do that to my red sweater?"

His voice echoes inside the dollhouse. "I never touched your sweater. You'd eat me alive if I came into your room."

"You used my sweater as a bath mat for your *Star Wars* figures."

Brian pulls his head out of the dollhouse. "You found my Stormtrooper and Jango Fett?"

"Found 'em, all right, along with Luke Skywalker, whose lightsaber has totally ruined my sweater." I can feel my nose flaring, and I'm ready to spit dragon fire. My brother does *not* bring out the best in me.

"I was scared I left them in Denver and I'd never see them again," Brian says. "Dad gave 'em to me for my birthday. Anyway, I never touched your stupid sweater."

"You're lying."

"Don't say that ever again!"

"I know you did it. It's going to take every penny of your allowance for ten years to buy me a new sweater. Starting today. Turn it over," I command, palm out.

A familiar voice hisses, sharper than ever, "Such an angry girl."

I spin around. "Stop it! Where are you?"

"Right here, can't you see?" Brian yells.

"Angry, angry girl." It's another voice, reedy and high-pitched.

"I AM NOT ANGRY!" I shout, then hear "Tsk, tsk."

Brian asks, "Who you talking to?"

"No one." Them! Could the day get any worse? These voices are making me crazy, even if I'm not. All at once, everything becomes clear, the same way sun burns off fog. Last night I heard — or I think I heard — the dolls threatening revenge. Did they cause all these things to happen? The furnace, the boiling pots, the ruined sweater? Is it all somehow connected to my afternoon with Dad? No, it can't possibly be. Why would it? I brush the idea off like it's just a crumb on a place mat.

Then my heart skips a beat and seems to stand still as a terrifying thought grips me by the throat:

It's going to get a lot worse.

When Dad pulls into our driveway, I'm dying to run right out and hop on the hood of the car and lie on my stomach, staring into the windshield at him, which will make him honk the horn until I roll off. That's what I used to do. I don't now. As soon as I see his car, I dart into the kitchen. In fact, if I didn't think I'd look stupid, I'd hide under the table. Brian is at his new Cub Scout den meeting, so that leaves Mom to open the door when Dad actually rings the bell. The man who lived with us all my life is ringing the doorbell at our house like company.

Peeking out through the swinging door, I see that Chester's nipping at Dad's shoes, and his tail is wagging like crazy. I guess dogs miss people, too. Dad kneels down and scratches Chester behind the ears. Mom doesn't invite him in, and after a couple of awkward minutes, Dad says, "Mind if I take Chester out for a walk while Shelby's getting ready?"

Mom hands him the leash that hangs by the door, and Chester's tail is already wagging so hard that it's slamming against the wall.

Dad says, "I'll bring him back in fifteen minutes or so, then Shelby and I can go have some lunch."

"Fine," Mom says. It's all so stiff and proper, like they just met at a funeral.

I hate this. I'm not going. I'd run up the road to Mariah's house, if I knew which one it was. Mr. Caliberti. I dash out the back door and run across the yard to his cottage. It'll be warmer than our house. I'll tell him Mom made soup for him, but it spilled all over the kitchen. I'll tell him about Sadie's notebook.

The ghost light's still shining when I bang on his door. Terpsichore glares at me from the window. There's no answer. Where would he go? He can't walk very far.

He doesn't have a car, and I never saw a taxi come for him. Then I remember he told Brian and me that he keeps an actor's schedule, goes to bed at five in the morning and sleeps until after noon.

I could hide in one of the empty houses up the hill, but they're probably locked up tight, and besides, even in the daylight they're creepy. Maybe I should hang out in the doll graveyard. Dad would never find me there. Like that's *not* creepy? I throw up my hands and slap my sides in resignation. There's nothing else to do out here in the middle of nowhere. Might as well go with Dad.

CHAPTER FIFTEEN

CHESTER AND DAD ARE BOTH PANTING WHEN they come back. They must have had a good run. I'm standing in the front hall with my jacket zipped up over my mouth. Dad puts one arm around me lightly, and I shrink away, but what I really want to do is pull his other arm around me so I can nuzzle into his chest.

"Ready to go, Shel?"

"I guess."

Watching all this, Mom says, "Brian will be waiting for you at about four." Then she sighs and returns to the kitchen. Chester looks from Dad to me and back. He must be totally confused. Can you divorce a dog?

In the car, Dad asks me, "Seat belt buckled?"

The best I can do is nod.

"The closest shopping mall is in Pueblo, about eighty miles away. But that's okay. It'll give us time to talk. Anything new with you?"

I shrug. We're not even out of the driveway yet and we've run out of things to say.

He keeps quiet, and I stare out my window until we get to I-25, and then words burst out of him, startling me so much that my head nearly hits the roof of the car.

"Shelby, let's get this straight. I'm your dad, you're my daughter, and we have to talk. Forget the shopping for a while. We're going to find a picnic table and sit down across from each other, and look at each other's faces."

"I don't . . ."

"Don't argue."

He swings off the road at a sign that says LUDLOW NATIONAL HISTORIC LANDMARK, and we drive in a half-mile over bumpy dirt. It's not a big fancy museum or anything, just a deserted spot out in an open field, with a few panels of dusty exhibit info — and a dugout where thirteen people suffocated during a coal miners' strike a hundred years ago. Great place to have a heart-to-heart talk, right?

He must have scoped it out on his way to Cinder Creek, because he leads me right to a picnic table under a big rickety tent, and he doesn't waste any time getting to the bone he has to pick.

"Mom tells me you've found a bunch of dolls at Aunt Amelia's house."

My radar's up. He's checking to see if I'm crazy. "Yeah?"

"And that these dolls are doing some curious things."

"Yeah."

"Will you tell me about it?"

I can't trust him, can I? I mean, he *left* us. But he's right there across from me, and his eyes never leave my face, and he's going to sit there for a week, a year, a century, until I open my mouth.

So I tell him about ugly, broken Miss Amelia; and Dotty Woman with her dandelion sprinkles on perfectly good food; and Baby Daisy; and the doll I locked in the drawer, Isabella, who might be Lady; and how the dolls don't stay buried; and about the dollhouse and the baby drowned in the bathtub; and about revenge and Sadie, who felt unloved, and her notebook and invisible writing; and crazy Emily.

It probably takes an hour telling him all this, and he never says a word, never laughs at me or frowns or snorts, though I hear his stomach growl. He just listens. When I've dumped it all out, especially the hardest part about the voices calling me an angry, angry girl, he reaches across the table and takes my hand. The wind is whipping around us, my nose is running, and my feet are Popsicles, but I don't care.

He's been quiet so long that his voice is hoarse when he finally says something. "You *are* an angry girl, Shelby."

My head snaps back. I thought he was on my side! But he's not through.

"You have every right to be angry, because I've done a terrible thing to you and Brian. There's no way I can make up for it, but I hope as time passes, you'll be able to forgive me and realize that I love you just as much as I ever did."

I don't want to cry. Tears are catching in my throat.

"It's a cliché. You know what a cliché is? It's something that's so common that it doesn't sound sincere anymore, but it's also true. Your mother and I got divorced, but I didn't divorce you and Brian. Do you understand that?"

"I guess," I mutter with a pout.

"Then that's a beginning of our long road back to each other."

He's still clutching my hand as I snuff back thick tears. "Crazy Emily's in a psycho hospital in Denver.

Mom says I need professional help. Do you think I'm crazy?"

"I don't. I believe all these weird things are really happening to you, but maybe there's a reasonable explanation that we just haven't come up with yet. Driving here today, I heard this amazing thing on the news about thirty-one South African elephants who walked miles and miles in single file, for days on end, to pay their respects to a man who'd died."

"What do some elephants have to do with anything?"

"A lot. The guy who'd died had devoted his life to saving elephants in the wild. Now, how did all those elephants know when he died? How did they communicate to one another that they were going to make this twelve mile pilgrimage? And how did they find their way to his house?"

"Maybe they're smarter than people think. Maybe they're smarter than people."

"Or maybe," Dad says, "there are just some things in this universe that can't be explained, like your dolls. Hungry? Me too. I read about a good Mexican restaurant up the road in Walsenburg. Wanna go?"

I nod. And back in the car, it doesn't feel as tense as it did when we started out.

Dad turns on the radio, and the car rocks with loud Spanish music to work up our appetites for enchiladas.

Dad and I decide not to drive all the way to Pueblo for a shopping mall. Besides, who shops with her father? So, while we're here in Walsenburg, we needle the car into the Crown Lanes parking lot and go bowling, like we used to *before*. It feels okay. Almost. Dad hurls that ball down the lane like he's trying to murder the pins and keeps getting a six-ten split.

After three games — me rolling my highest ever, a 114 — Dad drives me back to Cinder Creek to trade me in for Brian.

I'm shy about asking, but I do it anyway. "When are you coming back?"

He's got Brian's stuffed backpack slung over his shoulder when he answers, "I'll talk to Mom. We'll set a weekend every month, how 'bout that? My six-ten split needs some serious work."

I'm smiling when they pull away, and then my heart goes empty because it'll be a long time until I see Dad again, and I'm churning with jealousy that Brian gets him for the whole night.

Once they're gone, I head back to Mr. Caliberti's cottage. Still no answer. Terpsichore doesn't even come to the window to glare at me. There's only one place they might be. At the doll graveyard I find Mr. C pacing back and forth, stabbing the ground with his cane, with the cat marching right behind him.

His back's to me. "Are you okay, Mr. Caliberti?" I ask as I get closer.

"Well, look at it!" He points at the little half-circle of graves. A gasp escapes my lips: Every single grave's been dug up, and each one is empty.

The dolls are gone.

CHAPTER SIXTEEN

MY HEAD'S THUMPING WITH RAGE. WHO WOULD do such a terrible thing? My hands shake like Aunt Amelia's used to, and I feel hot blood stampeding through my veins. "Did you do this, Mr. Caliberti?"

"Child, these old bones could not lower themselves to the ground for such high jinks and rise to tell about it. Do you see me up on my feet?"

Terpsichore is wound around Mr. Caliberti's leg. That skinny cat couldn't have done this much damage. Not even a big dog like Chester could have done it. Brian? That first day, when we reburied the Miss Amelia doll, and she somehow got out of the grave and up into the dollhouse — well, it's possible Brian dug her out. He said he didn't, and he seemed just as surprised by it all as I was. No, not even Brian would do this. But then, who did?

"Where are they, Mr. Caliberti?"

"A veritable conundrum."

Whatever that is. The dolls must be up in the attic, but how? And more importantly, why? "Sadie's doll-house, I'll bet that's where they are."

"Sadie's legacy lives on," Mr. Caliberti says with a sigh, and Terpsichore whines in agreement.

Letting the screen door slam good and solid, I fly into the house, almost past Mom, but she just *has* to trap me.

"How was your afternoon with your father?"

"Fine," I say.

Mom twists the dishcloth in her hands and stares me down. "Did you tell him about the dolls?" I can't tell if she's just worried about me, or if she's really worried I'll stop hating him and she'll lose me.

"He *gets* me, Mom. Unlike you, he doesn't think I need a head doctor."

Her face and shoulders sag. Oh no, now I've hurt her feelings. I reach out to hug her, and she pulls me tightly against her. I can hardly breathe, but it's been a long time since she's hugged me this hard. When I pull away, we both have tears in our eyes.

"I need to go up to the attic," I tell her softly.

"Sure, honey, go on."

The day's shadows have fallen, and the attic is darker than ever. Why didn't I grab a flashlight? I tilt the open side of the dollhouse in front of the window. Furniture slides around, a bedspread falls off, a tiny chandelier sways — but the bathtub's dry with no baby facedown in it. No one stands by the window watching for us, or sits at the kitchen table waiting for breakfast. The house is totally deserted.

So where are the dolls?

"MOM!" I yell, jumping down the last rungs of the ladder with Chester nipping at my heels. "Do you know anything about the dolls from the graveyard? Did Brian bring them in here and hide them as a big, fat joke?"

"If Brian brought them in, I didn't see it happen," Mom says, "but I have good news for you. Your UV penlight came earlier than expected while you were gone. Now you and Brian can get your cryptology project going before school starts on Tuesday. Maybe you can get extra credit for it in science. The box is on your bed."

I make a beeline for my room, with Mom right behind me asking, "Where are the shopping bags?"

"We didn't go to the mall." I open my door, and there's the box tantalizing me, but Mom wants to talk.

"How did you spend all those hours?" she asks.

"Bowling."

"No new school clothes? Figures," she mutters. "You can always count on Sam Tate to do the right thing."

I tear open the box and read the instructions. It seems simple enough, even for somebody like me who's not too technologically gifted. I'm sure not waiting until Brian gets home to get right into Sadie's notebook.

But that turns out to be another slow process, moving the pen from word to word like somebody who's just learning to read. Worth it, though, because I'm getting lots more info on the Tasmanian she-devil, Sadie:

Mother dotes on that bleating little pink thing she's calling Baby Daisy. Just plain Daisy would be enough, wouldn't it? Or how about Duz? Mother kisses her wrinkled forehead and nose and pulls her close and is all smiley for a change. What is so special about a baby? I'd rather have a cocker spaniel puppy to keep Plumy company. Dotty and Celeste and Amelia and all the rest of them, except Father, who's in Romania, they can't wait to get their hands on that shrill Baby Daisy, while I'm invisible over here, even with Plumy on my shoulder squawking, and even though my face is flushed with fever. Dotty Woman has laid a cool cloth across my forehead that makes me shivery, and my hands shake as I write in my journal. No one notices, Mother least of all.

Oh, mercy me, HE just came in with a bunch of daffodils from the garden, and he DOESN'T EVEN LOOK AT THE BABY!!!! He nods toward me and says, "Morning, Miss Sadie," and my heart flutters wildly. But then I see the way he lowers his head and shifts his eyes toward ugly Amelia's back. I hate them all, every one of them! Whatever this illness is that's plaguing me, I hope they all get it even worse!

Poor Sadie must have been pretty sick, and I feel sorry for her, but to wish it on everybody else? This word-by-word thing is making my eyes sting, and so are Sadie's selfishness and rage. I have to quit for a while, but then the pen slides across another few words and my breath catches like it's stuck in my chest:

. . . I ripped Amelia's head off and tossed it under Father's car when Dotty wheeled me

*out for a morning walk, and I feel so much
better now!*

I'm ping-ponging back and forth between sympathy for her and anger. My stomach flip-flops the same as it does when there's a sudden dip on a Ferris wheel. This afternoon's enchiladas burn in my throat. What kind of horrible person was Sadie that she'd rip a doll apart and throw the head under her father's car? That's brutal and heartless. But the diary says poor Sadie was in a wheelchair. I don't know what to think about her.

Gets me wondering if I've ever been mad or upset enough to rip a head off. Not exactly, but my memory circles back to the scene I hate to watch on the screen in my own head: Dad's wedding in July.

I said a team of horses couldn't drag me to the wedding, but I went. Even Mom said I should go because the ceremony was a piece of my own future. There was no big white gown, no walking down the aisle, no flowers and organ, no wedding cake. Just all of us standing in the office of Terri's minister, Dad holding Brian's and my hands, and Terri holding Marcus's hand.

Uncle Garrett, Dad's brother, stood behind us, next to Terri's mother, while Pastor Rhoda beamed at all of us. I felt frozen like a statue in the park. If you threw pebbles at me, I wouldn't have flinched. The only good part was that Pastor Rhoda didn't say, "You'll be one big, happy family." What she said instead sort of made sense, and this is how I remember it and play it over and over again in my mind until it gets scratchy like one of Aunt Amelia's old records. She said, "Marcus, you don't have much experience with fathers, and you're used to having your mom all to yourself. You and Sam are going to have to learn how to swim these new waters together."

Marcus smiled, like he was pumped to dive right in. I didn't even want to stick one toe in the water. I was already drowning.

Pastor Rhoda put a hand on our shoulders, Brian's and mine, and said, "I don't know you as well as I know Marcus, but I want you to think about this in terms of the family groups you'll live in." She turned around and drew a circle on the whiteboard behind her and scribbled *Brian, Shelby, Mom* in it. She left a big space, then drew a *Brian, Shelby, Dad* circle. Okay, I got it so far, but it was the blank space in the middle that worried me.

"What I'm saying, Shelby and Brian, is that you will learn to navigate in all these circles, especially this new one." She wrote *Brian, Shelby, Dad, Terri, Marcus* and ran the chalk around and around that circle until it was the biggest and thickest of them all.

My heart sank. "Never!" I silently shouted, searching for Brian's eyes to make sure he was with me on this, but he wasn't looking my way. He was leaning forward around Terri to peek at Marcus, since he'd never had a brother before. I kind of stepped back a little and felt Dad's hand tug mine.

"I'm not saying it'll be easy," Pastor Rhoda told us with a sympathetic face. "But with patience and time, Brian and Shelby, and the loving guidance of both your parents, it will feel right, I promise."

"How can you promise?" I blurted out, and then I was so embarrassed that I felt my skin, head to toe, turning all shades of red. Terri's mother coughed, Uncle Garrett gently put his hand on my head, and Dad squeezed my hand.

Just like that, in about ten eye-blinks, Dad and Terri were married. To each other. Pastor Rhoda hugged each of us and handed us a card with a string of wedding bells at the top and silver printing that said:

Samuel Edward Tate

AND

Teresa Augusta Millard

WERE JOINED IN WEDDED HARMONY AT

MOUNTAIN VALLEY CHURCH

IN THE PRESENCE OF GOD AND FAMILY

Then we all went out to eat at a Chinese buffet, which was a good idea, because everybody trotted back and forth to the buffet so many times that we weren't all at the table at once and didn't have to make normal conversation. The egg rolls were greasy.

After dinner, Terri's mother whisked Marcus off somewhere, and Uncle Garrett took Brian and me home to Mom so Dad and Terri could go on a honeymoon. I hoped they missed their plane and had to sit up in the airport all night.

At home I tried to ignore Mom's questioning eyes and left her to wheedle the whole wedding story out of Brian. As soon as I was alone in the bathroom, I ripped that silvery card into a million pieces and soaked them in the sink, then flushed the whole pulpy mess down the toilet.

Which is why Sadie ripping that doll's head off reminded me of Dad's wedding.

The strange thing is that the Miss Amelia doll we found in the doll graveyard *does* have a head. Is it the same head? Same doll? She's ugly and roughed up, but she couldn't grow a new head like an earthworm does. Do you screw a doll's head on as if she were a bottle of salad dressing? Maybe I need to Google porcelain dolls.

Mom's in the kitchen, of course, so I flip open her laptop on the dining-room table and type in *porcelain doll heads.* . . .

CHAPTER SEVENTEEN

THIS IS SO WEIRDLY SICK. YOU CAN BUY *PARTS* for dolls. There's a really gruesome picture online of a human baby–sized porcelain doll, but it's in five disconnected parts. There's a bald head with a face that doesn't have eyelashes or eyebrows, two chubby arms, and two stubby legs, but no torso body section. It looks like the kind of crime scene you'd never want to see.

I also discover that their bodies are stuffed with sawdust and paper pulp and gluey gook, and I almost gag reading that animal bones are ground up in the clay that's used to make the dolls' faces and hands and feet. Kids *play* with these things? I'm beginning to think dolls are super weird, in the same way that clowns are supposed to look hilarious but are really scary and pathetic.

And yet, there's something so . . . human about these

mysterious dolls at Cinder Creek, something that tugs at my heart. How is it possible that they *know* how and why I'm mad all the time, when Mom doesn't seem to understand?

I keep reading about porcelain dolls, scrolling through dozens of pictures of sad and happy and broken and beautiful and scary and scared faces. But in all that online research, I never see a screw-on head the size of Miss Amelia's. Yet she has a head now. So what really happened to her? Was Sadie lying about ripping the doll's head off? Can I believe anything Sadie says in her journal? No question about it, I need to get more info from Mr. Caliberti.

I zip past Mom, who's playing around with her dehydrating machine for SerenaStockPot.com, and dash out the back door, which is the closest path to Mr. Caliberti's cottage.

He opens the door before I even knock and says, "Terpsichore and I are perplexed and aggrieved about those emptied grave sites. Are you as well?"

"I sure am. I'm wondering if you can tell me more about Sadie, and then maybe we'll understand what happened to those dolls."

"What information interests you, young miss?"

"Well, was she a big liar?" Oops, there I go, thinking with my tongue again.

Mr. Caliberti gazes up at the ceiling fan that whirs around and around, whistling quietly. "There are bold-faced fabrications, and there are harmless departures from the facts. For example, I have recently returned from Timbuktu."

"I thought you said you were returning from Kathmandu, or maybe Xanadu, not Timbuktu."

"Precisely."

I just shake my head in confusion.

"Kathmandu is a lovely city in Nepal, that is, Asia, and Timbuktu is an equally delightful city in Mali, which is in Africa. Xanadu is a phantasmagoric Eden. But does it truly matter which one I visited? All are faraway, exotic places with many splendors you have never known."

"Excuse me, Mr. Caliberti, but I have no idea what you're talking about."

"Departures from facts, and facts are not truth, my young miss."

"So, are you telling me that Sadie made stuff up, but she wasn't actually lying?"

"Am I? Why, how clever of me! More to the point, what I am saying, for example, is that my companion, Terpsichore, is named for the honorable Greek muse of the dance. Come, kitty, kitty."

The cat leaps off the mantel and takes a running dive onto Mr. Caliberti's lap. "There's my sweet girl." He nuzzles into her gray fur. Clear across the room I can hear her purring.

"I'm reminded of a frolicky old song you may not have heard. Here's how the chorus goes." Mr. Caliberti sings it in a deep, roaring voice, like it's opera:

Boys and girls together,
Me and Mamie O'Rourke,
Tripped the light fantastic
On the sidewalks of New York.

"They danced, the singer and his sweetheart, on the sidewalks of New York. Just picture that."

I've never been to New York. In fact, I am totally lost and starting to worry about Mr. Caliberti.

He's not through yet. "So, young miss, when I say that Terpsichore trips the light fantastic, am I honestly saying she dances? Or, more elegantly, that she is light-footed and graceful in her lissome movements?"

Yep, I'm pretty sure Mr. Caliberti has a few screws loose in his head. I think they call it dementia, when old people stop making sense. And *dementia* sounds like *demented*! Is he trying to tell me that Sadie was demented, in the same way that Emily was crazy, and that I'm going to end up like them because there's something sinister in our house that turns nice girls into lunatics? Now I'm terrified! I have to get out of here. As soon as I stand up, Terpsichore leads the way to the door. She wants me out of here, too. Why does Mr. Caliberti's cat hate me?

It's deathly quiet in the house with Brian gone. I'll never get over it if Dad took him bowling today, too. That's special for Dad and me.

Mom says, "Notice how nice and toasty it feels now? Odd thing. The heating man said there wasn't anything wrong with the furnace, but that the pilot light had blown out. You and Brian weren't down in the cellar messing around with it, were you?"

"Nothing could make me go down there!" I protest.

"Must have been a gust of wind," Mom says unconvincingly, since we both know that the cellar has no outside windows.

I think it was the dolls, up to their vengeful mischief, but I keep this to myself. Mom would freak if she heard me say it. I'm scraping the last of our chicken salad into a fridge container when someone knocks at our kitchen door. Mr. Caliberti's shadowy head is visible in the small window.

"We should have invited him for dinner," Mom says, taking out another bowl for strawberries in case Mr. Caliberti wants some.

When he steps into our kitchen, I'm shocked to see that his face is as white as Elmer's Glue. He's carrying a black trash sack bunched at the neck. It's big enough to hold a pony, but it's almost empty.

"Come in! Have some strawberries," Mom chirps.

Mr. Caliberti holds up the bag, rattling the contents that have sunk to the bottom. "I took the liberty of disposing of my humble garbage in the trash bin on the lot." He waits for some sort of reaction. Mom bustles around, clearing the table and stashing things in the fridge, while I wait to see what he's getting at.

His voice shaky, he says, "Terpsichore jumped into the trash bin and mewled so frantically that I felt compelled to investigate. This is what I found." The bag fans out on the table, scattering the salt and pepper shakers and a pile of napkins. Mom has her face in the pantry; I hear her sliding cans back and forth. Mr. Caliberti opens the sack with such drama that I can't resist peeking in over his shoulder — and gasp!

Inside the bag is a tangle of dolls.

Mr. Caliberti gazes into the dark bag. "Some heartless creature tossed these beauties away as if they were nothing more than unworthy refuse."

I don't have the heart to tell him that I've tried to bury them over and over again, because suddenly I realize that these dolls are more to him than just toys, that they represent real people he's cared for. Loved. His eyes seem to deepen with sadness as he says, "Who would do such a terrible thing?"

One by one, the dolls are lined up across our table, and Mom backs out of the pantry with a sickly look on her face.

"Mom! Tell me it wasn't you."

"I was so worried about you and Brian, with your wild ideas about these dolls, as if they had supernatural powers. And I felt you were getting dangerously attached to something that was pure fantasy. I thought if I dug them up and threw them in the trash before Tuesday's pickup, we'd be done with it all, and you could start school like a normal person."

"*Mom!*" I keep staring at those dolls on the table. There's Miss Amelia, looking totally worn out, and Baby Daisy, sweet and pink with the blue bow glued to her porcelain head. Next to Baby Daisy there's a boy doll I've never seen before, wearing an old-fashioned white sailor suit with one of those funny pointed sailor caps. His face looks very serious.

Mom sinks into her chair, bracing her chin in the V of her hands. "I'm sorry, Shelby. I thought it was the right thing to do — a mother's intuition."

Mr. Caliberti says, "But, my dear, they were not yours to dispose of."

"I suppose it was wrong, but done for the right reasons."

I can't believe she'd do this to Mr. Caliberti and me! Fighting back tears, I introduce her to each doll, so they'll be real to her, just as they are to him and me.

"This one is called Miss Amelia. She's Aunt Amelia, seventy-five years ago, kind of broken up because Sadie

Thornewood didn't like her. See the baby? Her name's Daisy, who was Sadie's little sister. Who's this one, Mr. Caliberti?"

"That's dear Dorothy Grabowski, Sadie and Daisy's governess. The kindest of souls was Dotty."

I flash on the grave marker, *Dotty Woman*. She's young, but she's in a black dress, old-lady black shoes, and a frilly apron. A stiff lacy cap sits atop her rolled-up hair that's the color of pink cotton candy. What's nicest about her is the wide smile that stretches across her cheerful face. Her eyes, though fixed in porcelain, are like twinkling little marbles.

"Who's the boy in the sailor suit?" Mom asks gently. I know she's trying to make up for tossing the dolls in the trash.

Mr. Caliberti lifts the doll that I'm now guessing is C.B. He closes both hands around it. "It is I, then known as Canby Berton, when my eyes first fell on the lovely Amelia Stanhope."

Mom gazes miserably at him and murmurs, "So sorry, so sorry."

"And this one is Betsy Anne," Mr. Caliberti explains. "Lovely thing, is she not?" Her big, blue, unfocused eyes stare straight ahead, perfectly round, with black pupil dots smack in the middle. Her mouth is open, silently singing. The eyes and mouth make her look forever surprised, shocked by something. She makes me feel uneasy, as if she disapproves of me.

Oh, like it's all about me? My mind kicks in with a picture of the doll graveyard. I remember five tongue-depressor grave markers on one side, and a larger, lonely stone marking Lady's grave across from the others. Six graves. But there are only five dolls lying side by side on our kitchen table: Miss Amelia, Baby Daisy, Dotty Woman, Betsy Anne, and C.B. We've never found Lady, either in the grave or in the house, but she makes six. Why is there no grave meant for Isabella, who's safely locked in my dresser upstairs? At least Mom couldn't get to her, since I'm walking on the key in my sock. It's curious that Mr. Caliberti never says a word about Isabella. Doesn't he know about her?

Then I think, *If Sadie stashed Isabella in the hatbox in our closet, maybe she never meant to bury her.*

Mom says, "One grave was empty, the one with the larger headstone opposite the horseshoe."

Mr. Caliberti nods in agreement. "That would be Lady's grave. No one's ever had the courage to entomb her." He looks puzzled for a moment, then says, "There ought to be an additional grave, an unmarked eternal resting place, not unlike the Tomb of the Unknown Soldier."

"Whose?" I ask.

"Ah, 'tis a mystery," says Mr. Caliberti. "Sometimes it is occupied, sometimes it is not." He fixes his eyes on mine with such intensity that I have to turn away or they'll burn holes in my face. "You will understand in the fullness of time, young Miss Shelby."

That's what Aunt Amelia said, that we'd understand in the fullness of time, but what does that *mean*?

Mom's bursting with questions. "So, if Miss Amelia represents our aunt when she was a girl, and Baby Daisy is Sadie Thornewood's little sister, and Dotty is the governess, and C.B. is you, Mr. Caliberti —"

He beams with pride. "I was a handsome devil, was I not?"

"You were. You are," Mom says. "But who is, or was, Betsy Anne?"

I'm wondering that, too.

"Good of you to ask. Betsy Anne was Sadie's better self. She is the avatar of all of Sadie's best qualities, the ones she was never able to show the rest of us because she was so haunted by the lack of love. Her father traveled the world, don't you know." Mr. Caliberti looks at me, and a half-smile forms on his lips. "He traveled from Kathmandu to Timbuktu to Xanadu, and had no time for Sadie. Mother Thornewood was a cold codfish, unlike my Amelia, whom I would describe as fried haddock, all crusty on the outside, soft and sweet on the inside, and a little bony. No, Mother Thornewood's heart was pickled in icy brine. She never had a smidgen of love for her older daughter."

"How could a mother not love her own child?" Mom asks, her face pinched with bewilderment.

After a sigh, a long pause, and a couple of false starts, Mr. Caliberti finally says, "Sadie was not a lovable child."

"No such thing!" Mom cries.

Maybe there is. Maybe she was pure evil. But as quickly as I think that, I remember passages from Sadie's diary. She was sick, suffered horribly with headaches that wouldn't quit, and she was too weak to walk on her own. I'll bet deep down, she was just a lonely, scared kid, starved for love. How different from Brian and me, with our two loving parents (even if they don't love each other anymore). All at once I'm flooded with sympathy for Sadie. But those dolls she tormented didn't have any way of knowing the real, inside Sadie Thornewood. They hated her right back. Same for Emily.

It's not a bit fair, but now I'm going to have to make up for every awful thing Sadie and Emily did.

CHAPTER EIGHTEEN

I MEAN, REALLY, CAN ANYTHING ON EARTH BE worse than the first day in a new school? I'm in a long-sleeved, knee-length green tunic and black leggings and high-top sneakers, and no one's dressed like me, not even the newbie sixth graders.

Here at Enderbrook Middle School, eighth graders are the stars of the whole show. They know the local Enderbrook uniform: jeans and college sweatshirts and flats. They all have that Enderbrook strutty walk, and they do that stupid Enderbrook fist bump/hip bump thing. They know their locker combos by heart. And they think they're really hot because they say *hola* instead of *hi* or *hey*.

The sixth graders, of course, wander around in a fog in this big, wide Enderbrook world, but everyone's dying to help them. Since I'm in seventh, I'm not supposed to be confused in the building anymore, but I am so lost.

I'm the only new kid in my whole grade and probably the youngest seventh grader on earth, and there's nobody here to say, "Two miles down A Hall is Mr. Ebert's Language Arts class, but they changed the room to C Hall, and he pronounces his name AA-BEAR," which I didn't know until after I said "EE-BERTTT," like a total ignoramus.

At lunch, no one bothers to tell me that no seventh grader would be caught dead at the table by the patio window, where I've just plunked down my tray in a nest of eighth-grade vipers.

I hate this school.

Elbows on my left and right creep closer and *accidentally* dig into my sides, but where am I supposed to sit? When someone taps me on my shoulder, I nearly leap out of my skin. I think I recognize the girl from my math class. She balances her tray on one hand and crooks the index finger of her other hand, motioning for me to follow. What have I got to lose? I swing my legs over the bench and, of course, clumsily kick the person next to me, which makes milk slosh all over his tray. Before I'm even on my feet, the pointy elbows have moved in to fill the space I'd just occupied.

My rescuer says, "Seventh-grade tables are over here."

Her perky ponytail whips around her neck as she weaves and ducks her way through the roaring crowd and flying milk cartons and plastic sporks and leads me to a crowded table.

She issues drill-sergeant orders: "Make way for a greenie, troops." Nobody moves a muscle. They just look up from their pizza slices and wilted lettuce and orange wedges and squish together to make room for us. She rules, but I get a sense they're not happy about it.

Her spacey grin is full of metal. "Welcome to End of the Earth Middle School, otherwise known as Enderbrook. I'm Darcy, and you're not," she says. "So, who are you?"

"Shelby. Just moved here a week ago. Well, not *here* here. Up the road, to a place called Cinder Creek."

"You must be in the house that crazy girl lived in. Emily somebody."

"Smythe, yeah, that's my house," I say with a deep sigh.

"Truly true?" She yells across the table, "Hey, guys, this is Shel. She lives in the nuthouse at Cinder Creek."

Nobody seems impressed, but Darcy thinks this is big news. "That's the house with the dolls, right? The spooky ones?"

I'm dying to ask Darcy what she knows about Emily and the dolls, but before I know it, the bell rings for the end of the lunch hour — if you can call twenty-five minutes a lunch *hour* — and everybody's on their feet tossing stuff into the trash and clattering trays helter-skelter on a conveyer bell. I haven't even eaten a bite yet.

"Come on," Darcy says, pushing me through the crowd. "Where's your next class?"

I quickly check a note stuffed in my pocket. "Room twenty-six, B Hall."

"Better hurry, then. You gotta crawl through a rabbit hole to get to B Hall, then cross an alligator-infested moat." She sees the horror on my face. "Slight exaggeration. Room twenty-six is right around the corner. Catch you later, Shel." And she takes off down the hall the opposite way. I'm probably wrong, but it's remotely possible that I just made a friend. It's just that I don't like being called Shel, as in peanut. Only Dad is allowed to call me that.

❖ ◉ ❖

"How was the first day of school, sweetie?" Mom asks, scratching steel wool around a gigantic soup pot in the sink. Corn chowder: I can smell it. Ugh.

"Rotten. I got lost between my locker and the gym, so I was late to PE, and I wandered into an eighth-grade Algebra class by mistake, and nobody at Enderbrook wears black leggings, and I'm definitely going to have to get my hair cut."

Mom dries her hand and reaches into the tool drawer for scissors.

"Pa-leeze do not even think about cutting my hair like when I was a little kid."

"I was just getting ready to cut a bag of cookies open, Shelby," Mom says, obviously hurt.

Then Brian bursts in like a hurricane and clatters his Legos lunch box on the table. The new Brian, Mr. Motor Mouth, spouts, "Six guys from my Cub Scouts are in my class! And my teacher's a *man*, Mr. Burke. I thought all teachers were girls. School here's way cooler than in Denver," he announces, and I'd like to grab a handful of his coppery hair and give it a good yank. No fair that he's happy at school when I'm as miserable as a fly stuck in a spiderweb. Plus, we won't be going to Leaning Tower of Pizza, which we always used to do on the first day of school. If we left now, we might get there by breakfast, since Leaning Tower is about two hundred miles away. I hope Terri and Marcus choke on their pizza. Not fatally.

Just until they turn blue and Dad has to do the Heimlich maneuver, and everyone points and stares at them.

Mom snaps me out of my fantasy. "Did you meet anybody interesting at school, Shelby?"

"Sorta. Maybe? This girl named Darcy. She knows about Cinder Creek. She knows — knew — Emily, the crazy one who used to live here."

"It's not nice to call her crazy," Mom says as she cuts open a package of Oreos and tosses out three for each of us.

Brian stuffs an entire cookie in his mouth, then mumbles with a blackish tongue covered in it: "I told everybody in my class about those weirdo dolls. They all want to come for a sleepover and see if the dolls turn into zombies in the middle of the night."

"Brian!" Mom scolds.

I think I liked Brian better when he didn't talk. I snap off the top cookie and scrape the yummy white stuff with my teeth. Dad hates when I do that, but he's not here, is he?

"Mom, admit it, there is something eerie about those dolls," I insist. "Even Mr. Caliberti thinks so, and he should know because, remember, one of them is meant to be him, when he was a kid."

"Mr. Caliberti is a little . . . he's not entirely with it," Mom says. "Can we please put those dolls out of our minds?" She bribes us with two more cookies.

I think she still feels bad about digging the dolls up. Brian and I decided not to rebury them after Mom trashed them. Now they're sitting on the top shelf behind glass in the hutch in the dining room. This way we can all keep an eye on them so they can't wander off again, or cause any mischief. The Mr. Caliberti doll, C.B., is the only one standing, as if he's the sentry guarding and protecting the other four dolls. I can see them from where I'm sitting here in the kitchen. Nobody's vanished, I'm happy to report. But it still nags at me — they want revenge, they said so, and I know in my heart they're going to get it. But I don't know how.

Yet.

CHAPTER NINETEEN

WHO'S IN MY ROOM?! I JERK AWAKE TO THE
sound of someone calling my name.

"Don't scare me like that, Brian!" I growl. "Isn't
this house creepy enough without you sneaking into
my room before the sun's even up?" Rubbing sleep
out of my eyes, I look around, but there's no one in
the room.

I hear it again, a blurbbely voice that sounds like it's
underwater: "Shhhhhhelby . . . Shhhhhelby Constance."

Nobody's ever called me that besides Gram and Aunt
Amelia, and I'm sure they're not talking to me from
beyond the grave. So, then, who is?

"Who are you? What do you want with me?" I shout.

The voice is silenced. Maybe I scared her. Whoever. I
swing my legs out of bed, glancing at the clock. I've got
exactly forty-seven minutes to get up, shower and dress,
eat breakfast, and hop in Mom's car to get to school.

And then I hear that gurgly, waterlogged voice again: "Saaave Laaady."

"What? Who? Who's saying that?" Is it Isabella, the doll locked in my dresser? I open the drawer, unfold her legs, and smooth her fancy dress and hat. "What do you mean, Isabella? Or are *you* Lady? Is that why there's no Isabella grave?"

I can't believe I'm having a *conversation* with someone who isn't alive! Am I going crazy, like Emily? Maybe, but the voice answers in a piercing "NOOOOOO! SAVE LADY!" And it's not coming from Isabella.

I'm so confused, and now the room's silent except for the buzzing of a fly, one of the stubborn few that survived into fall.

"Shelby! Brian!" Mom calls up the stairs. "Breakfast is ready. French toast, your favorite."

I shake the cobwebs out of my head and try to convince myself I wasn't quite awake, that my unconscious mind was revving in overdrive, that it was all a dream.

It wasn't a dream, though, and now my heart's racing while my mind zips through a dozen troubling questions, like who Lady, the doll missing from the large grave, really is. Obviously, it's not Isabella, since I let her out of the locked drawer, and she's perfectly safe where she is now. But why does the real Lady need to be saved? And what does she need saving from?

But the biggest question is: How am I supposed to save her?

Mom's super chatty on the way to school. Second day at Enderbrook Middle. It's gotta be better than day one, right?

"You okay, Shelby? You seem a bit distracted."

A bit? Hah! My mind's eons away, wondering how I'm going to find my locker again and puzzling over the Voice begging me to "Saaave Laaaady," as if a life depends on it. But whose life — Lady's, or the Voice's? What's also streaming through my head is the fact that it is totally abnormal to hear voices, especially when they bring frantic warning pleas.

"I'm fine, Mom." I blow her a kiss and hop out of the car while she's barely slowed down. I can't handle any more questions right now, and I have to face a tribe of kids who wish I'd never moved to town. They're all loitering around the front steps, waiting for the first bell to ding-a-ling so they can swarm the halls.

Darcy's waiting for me, chewing on a piece of beef jerky. "Want a bite?"

I shake my head. Would I take a bite of something she's slobbered all over?

"Did you finish the math?" she asks.

"Oh, I forgot about it."

"Get to the library. You might be able to whip through it before the second bell, or during Homeroom."

Isn't she just a wee bit too bossy? Then she pulls a sudden switch:

"Have you noticed Arden Kells?"

"Is that a girl or a guy?"

"Omygawd, Shelby, you need to learn to tell the difference! He's only the cutest specimen in our Language Arts class. All that golden-blond hair that hangs over his gorgeous eyes, and he's taller than most of the seventh-grade gnomes. Look him over thoroughly at lunch, and then let me know if I should go for the gold."

The bell rings, and we all stampede inside. If I remember which way the library is, I'll at least get a start on the math. Darcy trots along beside me, and through the chaos of the hall I hear her say, "I'm glad you came to Enderbrook, because I've known everybody at this school *forever*. I need fresh blood." Then she peels off, pointing to the opposite end of the hall, where the library is. No time to do the math.

Most of the day's a blur, except at lunch I check out Arden Kells and flash Darcy a thumbs-up. No one else at the table is half as cute as he is.

❧ ◎ ❧

After school when Mom pulls into our driveway, she has to weave around a bunch of vans. "What's going on here?" she asks. Like I know?

I spot one panel truck with an extension gizmo on the roof, sticking up in the air.

"Oh, shoot!" Mom cries. "It's the *America's Most Amazing* crew Aunt Amelia warned us about." Cameras and cables and all kinds of electronic gear are smashing our front lawn and are strewn up the hill. A guy in baggy jeans and a T-shirt with the company logo splashed across his chest — CABLE 87: ALL GHOSTS ALL THE TIME — comes bounding toward us with a big grin on his face.

"Glad you're home. Mrs. Tate, is it? I'm Drue Kennedy, associate producer of *America's Most Amazing*. Double meaning, get it? America IS most amazing, which it is, and America's most amazing phenoms. Pretty clever, eh?" He sticks out a sweaty palm, which Mom ignores.

"You cannot shoot inside our house, outside our house, behind our house, or anywhere within a hundred feet of our house, and if you do, I'll get a restraining order."

"Whoa, Nellie! You're tougher than the old lady who used to live here! Okay, okay, I get the drift. No can do the weird goings-on in your house. No sweat. It so happens, we're hanging around waiting for clearance from the bank that owns those houses up the hill. The one on the right is freakin' Phantom City."

"It is? Why?" I ask, and Mom throws me a warning look.

"That guy who used to own all these houses . . . Thornewood? Long time ago there were live coal mines all over here. Thornewood had a monopoly on the ones between here and Trinidad. He got filthy rich on the backs of those miners who earned practically zilcho for their labors."

"Look, Mr. Kennedy —" Mom begins, but I interrupt her.

"So what happened in that house on the hill?"

"Okay, okay, so one of Thornewood's business honchos was living high on the hog up in that house. Then one day a couple of coal miners got trapped down in the nearby mines when a ceiling collapsed. One guy was rescued, but the other one, he died of some kind of gas poisoning 'cause he already had black-lung disease. Lousy ventilation down there."

"Very interesting, Mr. Kennedy, but we need to —"

"Wait, I haven't got to the good part yet. So, turns out he's been haunting that house ever since. The last three renters saw him, clear as day. Man, that's right up our alley at Channel 87! So here we are. Soon as the bank gives us the go-ahead, we're ready to roll."

"Is there anything weird about dolls in that house?" I ask eagerly.

"Shelby!"

"Dolls? Not that I've heard." He whips out a little notebook and jots down *DOLLS?* "Could be. We haven't been able to get inside yet. Official papers and all that. The network's skittish about breaking and entering," he says with a chuckle. "But, hey, I'm on salary. I've got all day."

Mom steers me toward our front steps and warns Drue Kennedy once again: "Restraining order, don't forget."

He puts his palms up and backs off. "Yeah, I'm cool with that."

I have got to get in that house!

CHAPTER TWENTY

Made it through the first week of school! But now winter has hit us with a foul spirit here in Cinder Creek. I remember reading at that Ludlow monument place Dad and I went to, that September of 1913 was one of the coldest in Colorado history. All those coal-mining families were striking. They were kicked out of their houses and lived in tents right out here on the prairie. Brrr! I'm grateful for the blazing fire in our parlor on this Friday night, even though I've been jittery about flames ever since Chester's doghouse caught fire behind our Denver house. Somebody carelessly tossed a lit cigarette in our yard. The little house that Dad built for Chester shot up in flames. Dad ran out and tamed the fire with a garden hose, but Chester was totally freaked. That's why he sleeps with us now, usually with Brian. It was two years ago, and I can still hear him howling as his house collapsed.

Gotta shake that off and think instead about the rich hot cocoa in my mug. Whipped topping floats on the chocolate and melts into cloudy swirls. Someone with more imagination than I have might be able to read my fortune in those swirls. Chester gazes up at me expectantly, as if I'm going to let him lap at my mug.

Mom's on one of the kidney-shaped couches, clipping recipes from a food magazine. Brian's on another couch peering at something on Mom's laptop screen. I'm sprawled on the third couch. I'm supposed to be reading chapter three of *The Giver* for Language Arts. But my mind keeps wandering to that house up the hill. How can I sneak into that creepy old place without Mom noticing I'm gone? The old-fashioned clock on the mantel says nine, and my eyes are starting to droop. Maybe I should go to bed, set my alarm for 3:00 a.m., and tiptoe out of the house without a single creaky floorboard giving me away.

That'll never work. Mom has radar; she'd bolt out of bed and catch me before the door closed behind me, and I'd end up grounded for the rest of my natural life. Here's a think-worthy question: If you're a divorced kid, and one parent grounds you, does the other let you go? Hmm. I'll have to test that one.

And speaking of Dad, I haven't been able to pry a single tiny detail out of Brian about their night together last weekend. Maybe it was terrible. Maybe it was too good to spoil by talking about it. That chills me, even though the fire is crackling away in the fireplace. I glance over at Brian. His whole forehead is wrinkled in concentration.

"What are you doing?" I ask, and not too kindly.

"Googling images to see if I can find out anything about that funny old pipe Aunt Amelia gave me. Here's one sort of like it." He turns the screen toward me, and Mom comes over to see the picture, too. It's a pipe a lot like Aunt Amelia's, with a painted porcelain bowl and a tassel.

Back to *The Giver*. Darcy said she read it in fifth grade, but it's worth reading again. Darcy, who's my maybe-friend. Darcy, who got to Arden Kells before I even had a chance.

I flop my heels down on the glass-top table. The dollhouse furniture inside scuttles around, and that one doll, the one that spooked me the first day in this house, isn't up to any mischief.

In fact, she's not there!

I pop forward to get a better look. My eyes scan the entire table up close, and there's no sign of her. Besides that, the bed she was lying in that was separated from the rest of the furniture is now shoved up between the wringer washing machine and the stove.

Brian! He's been shuffling things around under this glass top, but why? Or is there something unexplainable going on? Something *else* unexplainable, like the furnace pilot light and my red sweater and all those pots boiling over at the same time?

A figure under the glass catches my eye, a doll I never noticed there before. She's got straight brown hair that wisps over her shoulders and eyes that aren't blue, but aren't quite green or brown, either. They're hazel. Like mine. I scoot down to get a better look, and it's as if I'm Alice in Wonderland, shrunk to her size, staring in the mirror. She looks just like me, even the small brown birthmark on her left temple and the tiny space between her front teeth. I do not like this one bit; it's way too freaky. A pulse is thumping in my head, and now the fire seems much warmer on my face, as though it's notched up a thousand degrees.

Mom is in a totally different world. "This is so peaceful. I'm feeling so much more centered out here in Aunt Amelia's house," she says. "Except for that rigmarole about the dolls." That part she mutters under her breath.

I, of course, have the sharp hearing of an owl, so I catch every word and bristle with anger. For once I keep my mouth shut, and after a deep breath, I remind myself that Mom simply doesn't understand what these little doll creatures can do. The Shelby me-doll — what can I expect from her? Next chance I get in the parlor alone, I'm taking her out of the table and . . . and what? Rip her head off? No, I will not do such a vicious thing.

I might as well face facts. I'm not going to read *The Giver* tonight, not when I have so many other things pinballing around in my mind. Checking to see that Mom's absorbed in her magazine, I pull Sadie's notebook out from under the couch, along with the ultraviolet penlight.

Mom says, "Oh, I see you're into your mysterious cryptology project. How is it going?"

My back's to her; how does she know? When people get to be parents, do they grow radar eyes and ears that are hidden in invisible places, but always tuned up?

"It's going great. Brian and I are inventing a secret code." The white lie comes easily to my lips. But is she suspicious? I glance around and see her lick her finger to flip a few more pages of the magazine. She gazes into the fire with a more hopeful look on her face than I've seen since *before*. Almost makes me feel guilty knowing that the dolls are up to no good. It's just a matter of time.

Word by word I inch through the pages of Sadie's notebook. Most of it's just daily drivel:

- That the parrot named Plumy that her father brought her from London keeled over and died one day in his cage. Plumy? It's almost as dumb a name for a pet as Terpsichore.
- What she had for an afternoon snack, which she called tea.
- How she ripped out the seams of a new dress her father brought her from Paris and used the tatters as a feed bag for her pony, Bonita. She sure got a lot of stuff from Europe.
- How her headaches were getting worse, and she was dizzy a lot and spending more time in bed in a darkened room. Hmm, I wonder what was going on.
- How the chauffeur drove her alone to a doctor in Trinidad, which is pretty sad, because you'd think her mother would go with her. She never wrote a word about what the doctor said, just that she couldn't stop crying and even Dotty Woman couldn't comfort her.

I'm really feeling sorry for Sadie. Maybe I shouldn't read any more of this. And then a fragment of a sentence pops out at me:

... So nobody can play chess now 'cause I captured the queen and stashed her ...

The sentence drops off right there. I flip the page quickly, and there's no more of Sadie's writing, as if she were caught by someone — her mean mother? — or was scared to say any more.

The next page is blank, and the next, and the next, and then there's invisible writing again. I slide the pen-light over the words, surprised to see that they're in a different handwriting. Printing, actually, which tells me that it was written more recently than Sadie's words because kids like me print everything unless they have to write in messy, old uphill-slanting cursive for school.

It hits me suddenly: Sadie's journal has morphed into Emily's. It's Emily, not Sadie, who hid the notebook under the floor at the bottom of the stairs. I can hardly wait to read what she's added. Is Mom watching? She better not be. She always has to know every inch of my business. Can't she ever just leave me alone? I turn toward her and hear a strangled whisper of a voice: "So many angry girls. Angry, angry girls. Where is Lady? Find her. . . . Find her," the haunting voice begs.

Suddenly I'm way more freaked out than I am mad. "Did you hear that, Mom?" I don't want to lose it the way Emily did. I don't want to hear things that aren't there.

"Hear what, the delightful crackling of the fire?"

The next thing I know, I'm up in the attic, terrified! I don't remember leaving the comfy fire, climbing the steep stairs, pulling down the attic ladder, or opening the trapdoor, but here I am, clutching the diary. My heart's hammering. Tears pound behind my eyes. I don't want to let them spill, even though I'm wondering, *Is this what it's like to be crazy?* Normal girls don't end up in places they can't remember getting to.

Is Lady up here? Is that why I'm here? I pad around on the floor feeling for something, but I don't even know what — a bump? A secret panel? A puddle? There's nothing. Besides some empty cardboard cartons, the dollhouse is the only thing in this bare space, and I slide on my rear over toward it. There isn't enough light to see in clearly, but nothing seems any stranger than usual.

"Lady? Are you here somewhere?" The pleading

voice I've been hearing is silent, but is that because I'm hot — dangerously close — and she's scared? Or because I'm so cold that she isn't wasting the energy begging me?

Frustrated, I crawl over to the window, hoping for a breath of air, but of course, the window's sealed shut. Up the hill, there's the shadowy outline of the two empty old Cinder Creek houses. The house on the left looms dark and skeletal as always, but the house on the right?

A light glimmers in one of its windows!

CHAPTER TWENTY-ONE

SOMEBODY'S IN THE HOUSE ON THE HILL! MAYBE it's a cameraman from *America's Most Amazing*, but why this late? And wouldn't he need lots more blazing light than just one dim bulb on the third floor? Besides, I don't see the TV truck with all the cables.

I think it's a regular person in there, but who? No one else lives nearby. Could it be a homeless guy who just wandered in? If I tell Mom, she'll want to take him a steaming bowl of vegetable soup. I'm going to keep an eye on that light while I delve into Emily's part of the diary. Maybe it'll give me a clue about Lady. Just gotta hope the penlight doesn't run out of juice. It actually works better up here in the dark, and I speed across whole sections of Emily's tiny printing. I picture her writing in this notebook while her family is nearby. She's scratching out each word in this cramped style so no one

can read it over her shoulder before the ink dries
invisible.

APRIL 20 – This is the true and honest diary
of me, Emily Smythe, age twelve-going-on-eighteen,
miserable citizen of this house of shape-shifting
hobgoblins that reign supreme. People don't count
a bit here. That's what Sadie Thornewood said,
and she should know because she's dead, dead,
dead, like Lady. So, Secret Eyes of the Future, if
you've found this in my amazingly clever hiding
place, and you're brilliant like me and can figure
out how to read words that aren't there, burn
this and GET OUT AS FAST AS YOU CAN!

Boy, Emily Smythe was sure conceited, and what a
drama queen. But should I follow her advice? Not yet. I
need to know more.

If you're stupid enough to keep reading, you
might find some things Mariah told me about this
oddball house interesting. Warning Number Two –
pay no attention to what Mariah thought because
she's a loony bird.

162

Mariah! The girl who brought the disgusting kidney pie. This is curious. Mariah stood right there on my porch and told me that Emily was — what's the word she used? — *loopy*. But here Emily's telling me that Mariah is a loony bird. Which one's lying, or are they both crazy? I quickly scan the next few lines and skip over to the next page.

APRIL 22 – Mama says I'm spoiled rotten, like sour milk or rancid butter, but Daddy knows me better. He calls me Cupcake and says I'm not spoiled, I just like nice things. My Shetland pony is way more adorable than Sadie's mangy old Bonita. I saw her horse in a picture before I burned up all of Sadie's albums. Low-class horse if I ever saw one.

I sure wish she hadn't burned Sadie's albums. Wish I could have seen her pictures to understand her better. I guess I'm the Secret Eyes of the Future, which makes me feel a little itchy, as if I have no business reading Emily's private words. But I can't resist.

MAY 3 – I'm way too old and too sophisticated to play with that dollhouse Mama insists we keep in the front parlor. Her bridge ladies get a buzz out of how it's an exact replica of the house we live in. Just about every dummy – that's a bridge term for the person who sits out after the cards are dealt and the hand is bidden, but they're all dummies, if you ask me – gets down on the floor and oohs and ahhs about the itty-bitty furniture and the eensy-teensy dishes and the utzie-cutsie dolls. They don't know that those dolls are pure evil.

Yes! Emily knew it. Wonder what the dolls did that convinced her. I skip ahead a few more pages. More about Mariah.

Mariah and I had a funeral yesterday. Buried five of those creepy dolls out in the field. Mariah's grandmother said some nice words that they didn't deserve, after all the awful things they did, but Grandmother Truva is sort of a minister, so she has to say nice words.

Odd. I had the impression from Mariah that her grandmother had passed away. I try to reconstruct our conversation, but it's muddled in my memory. Something about "before she left this world a few years ago." Yes, now I'm sure of it, because I told her I was sorry for her loss. Hmm.

Then we stuffed all five dolls in the ground in their very own graves and covered them with mud and rocks and weeds and dead fish and glops of algae from the pond, and coffee grounds and wads of honey-soaked paper towels, and that was the end of the dolls. "Hallelujah." That's what her grandma said at the end of the service, and Mariah and I shouted it right back at her. Hallelujah, baby!

But I'll bet they didn't stay buried. Yep. Three pages later, Emily writes:

I cannot believe it. All the graves are dug up and empty, but I know where those dolls are. This morning I kneeled in front of the dollhouse, shivering and quivering, and verified my theory. The dollhouse was full of those creepy dolls, the ones we buried and lots more. They're multiplying like rabbits! I shook the house, and they all toppled over and scattered. Except one. It stopped me cold to find a new one that looked just like me! And she was lying in the bed of the bedroom just like mine, under a patchwork quilt just like the one I brought from our last house, the NORMAL house we used to live in before Mama and Daddy had the insane idea to simplify our lives by moving out here to Nowhere, USA. I'm sure that that patchwork quilt wasn't in the house before, so who put it there? Only one suspect: that grouchy old woman, Amelia What's-Her-Face, who lives in the cottage out back.

Aunt Amelia? Was she involved in the evil things these dolls did during Emily's time here? I wish I could talk to her about it, but of course, she's gone now.

It's just the kind of thing the old bat would do, digging up the graves. Hilarious to think of her plowing through all those coffee grounds and mud and honey! But just as I was having a good laugh, the doll with the gorgeous blond hair to her waist, opened her expressive blue eyes (like mine!)

and I swear, she stared right at me as if she knew me and hated my guts.

I can understand that. I sort of despise this conceited, obnoxious brat myself. Who was worse, Sadie or Emily? I keep reading.

I couldn't help myself. I grabbed that doll, ripped her head off, and threw her across the parlor. Her body scooted way under the green couch, and her head bounced under there after her. It felt so, so, so healthy. That's when I had another of my superlatively awesome ideas. Can't wait to tell Mariah about it. I'm going to rip off an arm or a leg or a head of a different doll every day, especially the bigger ones, the ones piled in the cradle up in the attic.

I search the dark space. There's no cradle up here, no big dolls. My eyes race over Emily's next horrifying words:

I'll dump each torn-off part on crabby old Amelia's cottage porch, or maybe I can sneak into *the place when she's having her daily constitutional walk and toss the parts on her bed, one each day. Oh, yeah, that will feel delicious, and it'll send the old witch into fits!*

"Angry, angry girl," I hear in a raspy voice, different from the ones I'm getting used to. This is the voice of the me-doll that Emily totally destroyed; I'm convinced of it, and she's letting me know that the dolls aren't through with me yet. That somehow I'm going to pay for the abuse Sadie and Emily heaped upon her and her companions.

Unless I can find a way to stop them. But I haven't got a clue how to do that. Well, maybe one clue. It probably has something to do with finding Lady. But that's as far as I get. Ugh.

My eyes are tired and dry from reading with this penlight. When I turn it off, I'm plunged into darkness like in a cave. One summer, the four of us, when there were four of us, went to Carlsbad Caverns in New Mexico. It's dimly lit for tourists, but for about two minutes they turn out every single light, and it's so deeply dark that you can't see your hand in front of your eyes.

Up here my ears have to be my eyes. I hear every creak of the floorboards, the scurrying of some sort of animal across the floor, probably a mouse, and an owl outside. You hear owls but don't ever see them. Maybe now I'll catch sight of one in a tree right outside. So I peer out the little window, and just then the light in the house on the hill winks out. Outside, it's totally dark, too, because the moon's hidden behind some trees. But after a few seconds I see the skeleton of a cottonwood that didn't survive the summer drought, and I keep watching for big, round, glowing owl eyes and will probably faint dead away if I actually see them.

Something's moving out there! A figure darts past our house, crouches under our downstairs windows, then stands again to hurtle down the driveway. I can't make out who it is — someone kind of tall, but slim. Large kid? Small woman? Definitely female because of the knot of wild hair on top of her head.

Mariah! I'm chilled to the bone to think that she was in the greedy coal baron's house on the hill. The *haunted* house, where she had no business being, and is now sneaking away from. Why? And why would she tell me that her grandmother died years ago when she was obviously still alive a few months ago when Emily wrote in the diary?

Tomorrow I'm trouncing right up to the Keystone Duplexes a half mile up the road, and I'll traipse back and forth all day until I find her house, because I have a few million questions to ask Mariah-not-Maria O'Donnell.

CHAPTER TWENTY-TWO

THE VACUUM CLEANER IS WAILING INSIDE WHEN I lean on Mariah's doorbell to make it heard. All the way to her house I practiced what I wanted to say, and what I shouldn't say. I'm sure not going to tell her that I found Sadie and Emily's diary. I'm going to start out slow and noodle my way into the real reason I'm on her doorstep.

But when I hear the vacuum turn off, and she's standing at the open door in a granny nightgown that brushes the floor, I blurt out the very thing I never meant to say. There I go, thinking with my tongue again.

"Why were you sneaking around my house last night?"

Mariah takes a moment to let the surprise roll off, and then spits out a lie. "I wasn't. I was here all night babysitting."

"I saw you! You were up in the house the *America's Most Amazing* people are taping. I watched the light go off, and then saw you slinking down the hill, past our house. I know it was you!"

She spins around and turns the vacuum on again, leaving me shouting into the noise, so I bend around her and turn it back off.

"We need to talk."

"You need to. I don't."

"Tell me about Sadie."

Her eyes widen, and she stares me in the face when she says, "She died."

"When did she pass away?" It sounds so much gentler than *died*.

"When she was eleven," Mariah says, watching my face for reaction.

My hand claps to my mouth. I knew she'd been sick, but sick enough to die? "How? What happened to her?" I mumble the words through my fingers.

After winding the cord on the vacuum, Mariah sinks to the bottom step in the hall, the nightgown stretched across her knees. "Depends who you ask."

"I'm asking you."

"Couple of theories. One, she had a kink in her brain,

a tumor or something. Gave her lots of headaches. Maybe it exploded in there." She points to her own head.

I remember Sadie saying in the diary that the headaches were getting worse, that she was spending more and more time in a darkened room. "And the other theory?" I urge Mariah.

"The governess."

"You mean Dotty?"

"She had this thing about dandelions, smashing dried flowers into powder to sprinkle over food."

"Dandelions aren't poisonous, if that's what you're getting at," I remind Mariah.

"Some flowers are."

"Don't tell me you think the governess poisoned Sadie with ground-up posie petals?"

Mariah shrugs. "Everybody knew about her weird ways. You gotta ask, how would a kid be alive one day, dead the next, when that governess never let Sadie take a breath without her?"

That's a think-worthy question. And here's another one: "How come you told me your grandma passed away years ago? I know she was alive just before we moved into the house."

"I didn't say she died."

"You most certainly did!"

"Anyway, she's my great-grandmother." Mariah squinches her eyebrows together in deep thought. Probably cooking up a new lie to pile on top of her other ones. "I'll bet I said she left this world a long time ago, right?"

"You did; that's exactly what you said."

"It's the truth. Since you're here, you might as well come have a glass of lemonade."

I follow her into the kitchen, where an old woman's sitting in one of those tilt-back lounge chairs, clutching its upholstered arms. Her feet are propped up, bare, with perfectly pedicured red toenails, which is a big contrast to her froth of wispy gray hair sticking out every which way. She doesn't look up or say hello, just keeps rocking her body back and forth.

Mariah taps her on the shoulder, and the old woman's eyes light up for a second, then go dim again. "Grandmother Truva, this is Shelby, from the Thornewood house."

She nods in slow motion. She looks alive all right, but just barely. Her face has no expression, and she seems to be chewing gently on her tongue.

There's just enough in the lemonade pitcher for a small glass for each of us. Mariah offers Grandmother Truva a sip, then motions for me to follow her back to the hallway steps.

"Was I lying? She has that Alzheimer's thing. She really did leave this world about four years ago. Just her shell's left."

I'm heartsick at the thought of the woman being so dead, yet breathing.

"Every so often she surfaces, like someone's flicked her ON-OFF switch, and she remembers her days as a preacher and says some pretty words from the Bible, but then a minute later she's gone."

"Oh, I'm so sorry."

Mariah shrugs again, which seems to be her favorite thing to do. "Could be worse," she says, gulping the last of her lemonade.

Then there's nothing more to say about it, and it's embarrassing sitting there on the steps in silence, so I ask, "What else can you tell me about Sadie, about when she died?"

"It was almost eighty years ago. What difference does it make now, and why should you care?"

Her question is blunt and bruising, and I feel snap-pish. "Then tell me about Emily."

Mariah raises one eyebrow, so I push on.

"Emily and the doll graveyard."

"I already told you. The girl is loopy, locked up."

"Yes, but —" Do I dare mention this? She'll wonder how I know. "But there was a funeral."

"Was there?" Another shrug.

"There must have been. You don't just bury a bunch of dolls without some sort of important words. Just guessing, here."

She's looking away from me, her face as expression-less as Grandmother Truva's.

"Maybe I'm loopy like Emily," I begin carefully. *And a loony bird like Mariah*, which I don't add. "It seems to me that those dolls are having a real hard time staying dead and buried."

Mariah bursts out in a loud laugh. Too loud to be natural. She's hiding something really big, I'm sure of it now. Some deep, dark secret about Sadie, or Emily, and who knows what else.

So I backpedal to play it safe and easy. "I know it sounds insane, and I don't really mean it."

"Hope not," Mariah says shortly.

"One more question."

"You're full of 'em."

"About when Sadie died."

"That again?"

How to frame this question without totally ticking her off? "Is it true that Sadie's mother never loved her? Loved her baby sister more, and that's why Sadie was so warped and mean?"

"How should I know?" By now Mariah's got her knees pulled up to her chin, her arms clasped around her legs. Looks like she's trying to curl into herself. What's she hiding?

"Do you know anything about Sadie's mother?"

"Nope."

I want to say what those directors say when they're making a movie: "Come on, work with me, people." Instead, I say, "Nothing?"

Mariah suddenly thrusts her legs out. She's mad. I mean, I recognize *mad* when I see it. And she probably figures she'd better give me a nibble of info or she'll never get rid of me.

"Grandmother Truva said Sadie's mother was a cold, stuck-up snob who never got used to living out here in Colorado. She came from London. London, England.

Related to royalty, back a few generations. That's what she said."

Now we're getting somewhere! "Don't stop now."

"Wanted everyone to call her by her royal name."

"Not Mrs. Thornewood?"

Mariah blows out a puff of air. "Not good enough for her. Talk about stuck-up; she made everybody working in the house call her Lady Thornewood."

A gasp escapes my lips. Lady! There's so much more I want to ask, but Mariah's got her arms crossed around her waist. I can tell that her well has dried up, and I'm not going to get another drop out of her, so I mumble something about Mom needing me at home, and I get out quickly.

Lady! This is mind-boggling information! But what does it mean? As I'm slowly walking home, kicking it all around in my mind, I realize that I still have lots more questions than answers.

Also, it suddenly dawns on me, I never found out why Mariah was sneaking around the house on the hill last night.

The question at the top of my very long list is this: Was Sadie poisoned by her governess, the one she called

Dotty Woman? And if she was, was it accidental or deliberate?

Mom's left a pile of shirts and napkins on the ironing board, as a reminder that I still owe her some payment for the penlight. I hoped she'd forget. Well, if I prop the laptop up on the wide end of the ironing board, I can whip through a couple of shirts while I read about poisonous flowers. Brilliant idea!

Okay, there's a purple flower called belladonna. The name's too pretty to be poisonous, but it is, and it causes serious headaches, like Sadie's diary talks about. That's Suspect Number One. Foxglove is another possibility. Ooh, it's also called witches' gloves and bloody fingers. Very promising! Eating this innocent-looking pink flower gets you a racing pulse and serious mental confusion, such as *thinking* dolls are talking to you or moving around on their own steam.

Steam! I've scorched the cuff of Mom's silk blouse. Just as I close the laptop so I can try to fix it, I see a few more words about foxglove: It can kill.

CHAPTER TWENTY-THREE

"TOO BAD ABOUT THE MISSING QUEEN," BRIAN says, fiddling with the odd chess set in front of the portrait of Mrs. Thornewood. *Lady* Thornewood. "This would be a fun set to play with, the way the pieces snap into place. But the game's no good without the queen."

Brian is obsessed with chess. Ugh. He's practicing for a tournament next month in Colorado Springs. He'll probably be the youngest player in the whole contest. Mom's driving us as far as Pueblo, and Dad's picking us up and taking us the rest of the way. That's what divorced kids do; they get passed from one snarly parent to another in parking lots. Will I ever get used to this?

I'm taking another stab at *The Giver*, because I have to come up with some kind of a project by Friday. I love the book, but my mind is buzzing like it's full of bumblebees. Belladonna. Witches' gloves, bloody fingers, flowers that kill. Someone had to pick them and feed them to

Sadie. Who? Why? Or maybe it never happened that way, and she died of some awful disease. It's all swirling around in my head, but I have to put it out of my mind for a while, because this is *the* night. I'll try to stay awake until a full hour after Mom goes to bed, and then I'm breaking out of jail and trekking up the hill. In pitch-dark, without a flashlight, in case Mom's still awake.

Brian goes into the dining room, where I hear the key turn and the glass door of the hutch creak open. *Don't let the dolls out!* I whisper. They've stayed locked in there for days already. Looks like we've finally figured out how to trap them — or are they just waiting for the right opportunity to spring free?

He comes back into the parlor with the smallest of the dolls, Baby Daisy.

"What are you doing with her?" I demand.

"Using her for the queen."

"No!" I snatch her out of Brian's hand. Her face is different from what I remembered. It used to be round and smooth, with rosy cheeks. Now there are cracks all around her eyes, the same way old people have wrinkles. The porcelain curls on her head are also cracked, and the sweet, innocent look in her baby eyes is replaced by an intense stare, with the eyes cast sideways as if she's scared she'll get caught.

Are the other dolls doing this to her? Are we, somehow?

"Won't work anyway. She's too big for the chessboard," Brian grumbles. "Gimme, I'll put her back."

"No, she's mine." Crazy as it seems, I'm thinking that if I take good care of her, she'll feel better. Her face will relax. She won't look haunted anymore.

Last year in school we did that thing where everybody got a five-pound sack of flour to take care of for a week. We drew faces on the sack, named our babies (mine was Kammie), and stayed with them twenty-four hours a day. Before I could eat a bite, I had to mash a banana for her and mix a bottle of milk formula. I kept her safe even while I was sleeping, careful not to roll over on her. That would smash the poor kid, and also send five pounds of flour snowing all over my room.

It was amazing how attached we all got to our flour sacks, but how easy it was to turn them into chocolate-chip cookies at the end of the week.

I'm going to do the same with Baby Daisy. Not the chocolate-chip-cookies part. I'm going to keep her with me no matter where I am or what I'm doing. I have a stretchy purple friendship bracelet that Evvie and Melissa gave me as a going-away present. "Our friendship stretches all the way to Cinder Creek and back," they promised, though they haven't even called me once.

I tuck the doll tightly under the bracelet on my wrist, palm side up. Baby Daisy and I are joined now.

I creep down the stairs in my socks, shoes in hand. There's not a peep from Mom's bedroom. Chester's snoring in his bed in the laundry room, and Brian's been zoned out for hours. Earlier, I oiled the hinges on the back door so I could slip out without any screechy sounds that might tip off Mom. I tie my shoelaces good and tight on the back porch, make sure Baby Daisy is secure under my bracelet, take a deep breath, and start out on my odyssey.

Good, there's a bright moon lighting up the path past Mr. Caliberti's cottage. His shade's open, and he's sitting in a huge easy chair reading a thick book. Terpsichore's on the windowsill, throwing me a dirty look as I slink past the cottage and hurry up the hill.

The higher I get, the more trees there are along the side of the road. One that's stubborn about giving up its fall leaves hides the moon, and I'm suddenly plunged into darkness. I've heard that if you lose one of your five senses, the others kick in, and now, since I can't see where I'm going, I hear every eerie sound — a branch bending in the wind, some kind of animal, maybe a rabbit or a roadrunner, slooshing through the bushes, a car way off down the road, insect song in the trees. I never noticed how noisy the silent night is.

Near the empty house, I stop and try to size up the situation. Half of me wants to run all the way back home, crawl into bed, and pull the covers up over my head. That's the smart half. The dumb half says, *Go for it, girl,* and so I do. I try the door; locked, of course. Did I expect this to be easy-peasy? I can't push up any of the windows, either. Maybe I'll have better luck around the back.

It's even darker back here, and I use the little pinpoint light of my ultraviolet pen to find my way from window to window. No way in. Some concrete steps trail down to the cellar. They're covered with decaying leaves and dead bugs that crunch on the way down. I spot a window open about a quarter inch that I can just get my fingers under to push up! The loud scraping sound sends some kind of animal streaking through the night, white stripe down its back. Skunk.

I climb in through the window and jump way down onto a cement floor, my knees throbbing from the impact and my heart pounding with fear. What if there's someone in here, maybe a homeless man who's squatting in this abandoned house, ready to spring at me like a coiled snake? What if this is the winter home of a family of wild coyotes? I dart around, pointing my penlight in every corner, and sharpen my ears to strange sounds. It's deadly silent. I creep from one end of the cellar to the other, guided by the puny glow of my penlight.

Something flies past my face close enough that I feel the windy flutter of its wings. How could a bird have gotten in here? I point the light toward the flying object, watch it close its broad wings over its startled night eyes. It's a bat! My heart stops for a few seconds until I can barely catch a breath. The bat flies out the open window, and I breathe again.

And then I see something else piled in a corner, arms and legs tangled together: broken dolls. Some with matted hair, some with missing limbs. One has no eyes, just empty black holes. Three heads without bodies have found their resting place in the stuffing that's hanging out of one doll whose seams are ripped open. One's head has a chunk missing, as if a wolf's taken a big bite, but, come on, wolves don't eat porcelain. Someone, a person, did terrible things to these dolls.

Sadie? Or was it Emily? Are these the dolls she wrote about in the attic cradle that isn't there anymore?

I'm sick to my stomach looking at them, dry heaves spazzing my body until I'm doubled over. Could Mariah have been looking for these dolls the other night? But why? And why didn't she take them with her? Maybe they made her as sick and bone-chilled as I feel, and that's why she left them.

Or maybe she never found them.

Is one of them Lady?

I point my penlight around, looking for something to give these mangled dolls some peace, some kindness. There's an old tarp, stiff with turpentine or something else that stings my nose. I smooth the canvas out and lay it over the mound of shattered dolls. It's not a proper funeral like in the doll graveyard that Emily wrote about, but it's a respectful burial just the same.

As I back away from the dolls, the penlight casts a thin beam in their direction. One leg suddenly shoots out from under the tarp! My heart rat-a-tats like a jackhammer.

The pile's just resettling, I tell myself. *There's nothing alive under there.* But even still, I hustle out the open window as fast as possible and dash blindly through the dark, all the way home.

Where Mom is waiting at the back door.

CHAPTER TWENTY-FOUR

"WHAT DO YOU THINK YOU'RE DOING?" MOM bellows.

Breathing heavily from running down the hill, I manage a spacey, "Woke up . . . needed some exercise."

"That won't do, Shelby." Mom's arms are folded over her waist in the *You are so cooked* position.

I collapse onto a kitchen chair and stretch my fuzzy mind for some explanation that she can live with. When my heart finally returns to a *thump-thump* that doesn't feel like it's going to explode like a bomb, I tell her, "I was curious to see what those *America's Most Amazing* people are looking for."

"At midnight? Alone?"

"Well, Mom, the ghosts only come out after midnight, right? I mean, haven't you read any scary stories in your life?" Oops, I'm starting to sound snarky.

"Sarcasm will not be tolerated in this situation, Shelby Constance." She sounds just like Aunt Amelia! She's still standing over me; seems like she's nine feet tall.

I ask, "How did you know?"

"Mr. Caliberti phoned me, bless his heart. Apparently Terpsichore saw you steal by his cottage and alerted him. He was worried." Mom scoots a chair close and sits down, throwing an arm around my shoulder. Tears mist her eyes. "I was, too. Anything's possible out here in the wild. I'm so relieved that you're safe and sound."

"I'm sorry, Mom." Now I've got tears in my eyes, too, and my heart is quietly thumping, remembering that I could have run into real danger out there.

"We'll talk tomorrow," Mom says, and it sounds like a threat. "For now, take off your jacket and I'll make you a hot cocoa to warm your bones."

I can't take off my jacket! First, the penlight might fall out of the pocket, and worse, she'll see Baby Daisy on my wrist. I'm just not ready to explain that yet. "I'm still kind of cold," I tell her, faking a shiver, though I'm sweating around the collar. I pull my arm below the table to feel for the doll snapped under my bracelet.

She's gone! I tap up and down under the sleeve, and

there's no little lump of porcelain. Must have dropped her along the way. I saw an Internet story about a divorced mother who kidnapped her son away from the father that had custody, and all at once a totally ridiculous idea pops into my head: The unnamed dolls piled in the corner kidnapped Baby Daisy, reclaimed her as one of their own.

I let her down. I've got to get back there to rescue her.

"Now," Mom says evenly, "what is the ultraviolet light for really?"

"The cryptology project!"

"Shel-bee," she says in that singsong warning way.

No use hiding the truth anymore. It's too much responsibility keeping it all away from Mom. "I found a notebook that's written in invisible ink. It belonged to Sadie Thornewood."

"Is that the woman who originally built this house?" Mom's dunking a tea bag into her cup, more a nervous gesture, I think, than a real effort to produce strong tea.

"Her daughter. This'll really break your heart, Mom. Sadie died when she was my age."

"Oh, dear God. What happened to her?"

I hear Mariah's words in my head, but not loud, like the dolls' voices, and I repeat what she said: "Depends who you ask."

Chester's awake now, and routing around for scraps on the floor. Then Brian stumbles into the kitchen, bumping into walls, all sleepy-eyed and groggy. "Whazzup?"

"Shelby and I were just having a late-night chat. Go back to bed, sweetie."

"'Zat hot chocolate? I want some, too."

The phone rings, sounding twice as loud as it does in the daytime, and Mom throws us a frantic look. "Who'd call this late? Your father?" See? He's still the first thing on her mind. She jumps up to catch the phone on the second bounce.

"Oh, thank you, Mr. Caliberti. Yes, she's fine, just a little impulsive." Mom could have said lots worse. "Well, certainly, if you'd like. None of us can sleep anyway." Covering the mouthpiece, she whispers, "He's on his way over."

We hear Terpsichore mewling at the kitchen door before Mr. Caliberti can knock. Chester wants to lunge at the cat, but Mom holds him back by the collar, and Terpsichore does her best to pretend Chester isn't alive. What a snob, that cat. She'd have been a perfect pet for Lady Thornewood.

Mr. Caliberti's in his red flannel nightshirt that nearly covers his leather bedroom slippers. He hangs his cane on the key hooks by the door and waddles to a chair. Mom slides a cup of cocoa toward him, another to Brian, and just about faints when Terpsichore leaps onto the counter.

"No, kitty girl," Mr. Caliberti scolds. "Only at our house, you know better." So the cat leaps from the counter onto Mr. Caliberti's lap and sniffs at the cocoa. He pulls the cup away just as she thrusts her pink, raspy tongue toward it.

While he's here, I might as well ask, "Mr. Caliberti, do you know Truva?"

"Truva O'Donnell? Certainly. Why, she must be a desiccated fossil by now. Old as I am."

Mom looks puzzled, but doesn't say anything.

"How do you know her?" My pulse races — I think I'm onto something important here.

"We were children together, before the Ice Age. Not so long ago, truth to tell." His eyes seem to be looking inward to a time far past. "She and my dear Amelia were the best of friends. Truva was around the house all the time."

"Did Sadie like her?"

Stirring his cocoa into dancing circles, Mr. Caliberti says, "Sadie liked no one except her parrot. The name escapes me." And then, I swear, he blushes! "And me. She fancied me. Well, I was a strapping young man then, why shouldn't she?" Terpsichore meows, either in agreement or in doubt, hard to tell which. "However, Truva had no use for Sadie, either. They were antagonists, as in the most serious theatrical performances."

Something's tugging at me — my conversation with Mariah about what happened to Sadie. "Mr. Caliberti, I told Mom that Sadie died real young. Could you tell us anything else about that?"

"She had severe, feverish headaches. Her eyes looked sunken in their sockets and white-ringed. She was white-ringed around her dry lips, as well. Very sick, the child was. I remember her lying on a chaise lounge in the parlor with a cool cloth pressed to her forehead. One day her frock had ridden up over her knees, and when I came into the room she quickly straightened it over her limbs. We said *limbs* in those days, not *legs*. Oh, she was sweet on me, yes, yes! But those headaches did her in."

"Were they migraines? A brain tumor?" Mom asks.

"Might well have been," he answers vaguely. "She wasted away shockingly quickly, in just a matter of weeks. After she passed, her mother keened and wailed for days."

"That would be Lady Thornewood?" I ask.

"Yes, herself. She had no use for Sadie until the poor girl went on to the next world, and then she nearly enshrined her daughter. Guilt, no doubt. Some say young Truva had a role in Sadie's death," says Mr. Caliberti somberly.

This is big news! Shocking. I wonder if Mariah knows. All *she* talked about was Dotty Woman as a suspect. I can't resist asking, "You mean Truva killed her?" Oops, another tongue-before-brain thought.

"There is no proof Sadie Thornewood was poisoned one way or another," Mr. Caliberti says, "but the rumor has lingered for years, like the odor of sharp cheese. I, for one, have never believed it."

Strange — he never mentions Dotty Woman as a suspect.

"What makes you ask about Truva O'Donnell, child?"

"I met her."

Mr. Caliberti's head snaps back, and Terpsichore falls off his lap. "She's still among us?"

"Just barely. She has Alzheimer's."

"I see." He scrapes his palm across his nighttime gray bristles on one cheek, then the other. "She used to make a special meat pie of some sort, I recall."

"Beefsteak and kidney?" I supply.

"The very one. I can still taste it."

"It was that delicious?" Mom asks doubtfully.

"That dreadful," Mr. Caliberti replies. We all laugh, except Chester, of course, who loved the pie Mariah brought us.

So, I'm thinking . . . if people have been hinting for three generations that Grandmother Truva was responsible for Sadie's death, it must be horrible for Mariah's family. Maybe it's all Grandmother Truva can think about, locked inside her own brain the way she is.

But maybe she *did* do it. Anyone can pick pretty, deadly flowers.

What if Emily told Mariah about Sadie's notebook, and she has reason to suspect that it's hidden in that house up the hill where all the dolls were tossed to molder? And what if Mariah thinks there might be a clue about Sadie's illness or death that would clear Grandmother Truva of the accusations? Maybe *that's* why she's been sleuthing around the abandoned house, trying to find that notebook before the *America's Most Amazing* vultures find it.

She doesn't know I have it! And she doesn't know that there's not a single clue about Sadie's death — only that her writing abruptly stops cold.

Mom and Brian and Mr. Caliberti are deep in some conversation that I'm paying no attention to, when I suddenly hear him say, "One day soon, Miss Shelby, will you take me to visit Truva? Perhaps I'll awaken some memories in her."

And help me solve the mystery. "Yes. I'd be happy to!"

CHAPTER TWENTY-FIVE

I CAN'T SLEEP BECAUSE MY MIND'S JUMPING LIKE kernels in a lidded pan. *Pop. Poppity-pop.* So many ideas bouncing around in there. And Brian's wide awake, too, so we might as well read more of what Emily had to say. We curl up on my bed, backs against the wall with Chester between us, and run the penlight over the next few sentences in the diary:

MAY 16 — Why would anybody in his right mind want to be a child psychologist? Mama took me to see Dr. Byington, whose office is full of toys that are way too babyish for me, and if you pick up a single one, he watches you like a hawk. I know that Mama betrayed me and clued him in about the doll dilemma at our house, because out of the blue he asked me if I like dolls. I used to, I told him, when I was maybe four, but I've outgrown them and I'm much more interested in getting a smartphone now and a bunch of apps, which Daddy's promised me next week. (Mama disapproves, but I always win.) Dr. B doesn't want to talk about cell phones. He wants to talk about dolls. I thought I was supposed to talk, not him! So he picks up this floppy doll that's the size of a Paddington Bear I used to have, and he pushes her toward me, but I yank my hands away, and the doll clunks to the floor. Ha! So funny! I can't stop laughing. And then I don't say one single, solitary word for the rest of the hour. Borrrrring.

"Does she sound crazy to you?" I ask Brian.

"I dunno. Maybe just like a spoiled brat."

I skim over a few entries that don't say much, looking for something about Sadie. Emily writes about her next visits with the psychologist, and how she turns her back and pouts and refuses to talk and even hears him doze off and snore. Finally we come to something meatier:

Dr. B asked me if I know what hallucinations are. Sure I do. They're seeing and hearing things that aren't there. So he asked me if that ever happens to me. I do *NOT* have hallucinations. I shouted it at him. They're not hallucinations if they're really happening, Dr. Dunderhead! I see those dolls shuffled from one place to another. THEY DON'T STAY BURIED!!!!! I hear them telling me they hate me. I even hear them scream when I tear their arms and legs off. It's really happening, Dr. B, and if you don't believe me, you oughta get some other kind of job, maybe a chimney sweeper or pool cleaner.

"She ripped those dolls apart?" Brian asks, horrified. He's such a gentle kid. He'd never hurt anything or anyone, even if he's an annoying pest.

And so I have to tell him about the horrible pile of broken, cracked, torn dolls in the empty house. "I'm guessing that Emily got in through the same basement window I did and tossed all of them in there to hide her nasty work, so she could visit it whenever she wanted to."

"Gross." Brian wakes Chester and gives him a big comfort hug. "Hey, what's that knocking sound?" Chester jumps off the bed and starts barking at my dresser.

"Just Isabella in the drawer," I casually tell Brian, as though it's no big deal that a doll is bumping around on her own. I don't even have to lock the drawer anymore. She seems happy just to be there. But she's driving Chester nuts. "Here, boy, come on back." He turns around and gives the dresser a suspicious look, but hops up on the bed, sending the bed springs squealing.

Brian seems okay with the drawer noise and says, "Sure are some spooky things happening with those dolls. Like the day we put them in the graveyard, and they turned up in the dollhouse in the attic. That was pretty weird, but we're not crazy." He glances at the drawer again for reassurance. "We're not like Emily, either, tearing those dolls apart like ripping up a comic book." He stops to think, nuzzling Chester, whose tongue is washing Brian's face. "Yeah, I think Emily is bonkers. I hope this doctor guy can get her over it."

I skip ahead a few pages in the diary to one of the last entries, written just two months before Aunt Amelia died and we moved in. Emily had stopped using most punctuation, her spelling was awful, and her printing was even smaller and more cramped, so it's hard to make sense of it:

There telling me abt Lady say I hafta find her
and free her they say it over and over again

slam my hands over my ears stuff 'em with coton
but still here them screeming at me louder and
louder and louder cant stop them what I do?????
Sadie same thing happen killed her it ll kill me you
hafta help me Dr. B HELP ME!!!!

"You think the dolls killed Sadie?" Brian asks, shuddering in total amazement.

I shake my head, but who knows what really happened? My blood runs cold, and at the same time, my palms sweat when I realize that both Sadie and Emily ended their diaries with desperate cries for help. Emily's next line is frighteningly short:

evil house God help nex grl here

"Oh, Brian, that's me! Us! We've inherited Sadie's and Emily's horrors."

Brian's face is pinched with worry, which worries Chester, too. He lays a reassuring paw on Brian's leg as Brian says, "Real life is sure a lot harder than chess."

I can't bring myself to tell him the hardest part — that the dolls are demanding that I find Lady and free her, just like they did with Emily. Will I be blathering like Emily in another month? Another day? Ugh. Double ugh. I've got to shake off that idea *right now*. If my little brother guessed any of it, it would totally freak him out. He's only nine. Let him stick with kings and pawns and worry about nothing more awful than the curiously missing snap-on queen.

Monday morning. Darcy's standing by my locker, slurping away on a chocolate Tootsie Pop. "There's a seventh-grade dance next Friday in the boys' gym. Let's go."

I panic. I don't dance. I have no sense of rhythm. I trip over my own toes. And gym floors are slick. I could slip and land on my butt and be totally humiliated. And does this mean dancing with actual boys of the opposite sex?

"Arden Kells is definitely going. He told Joel, who told Renée, and she emailed me last night with the news. So don't leave me there alone."

I have no idea who Joel or Renée are. They'll probably be at the dance with every other seventh grader on earth. "You won't be alone. All your friends will be there; you won't need me."

She nods, but then I see a wave flicker across her face and I realize the truth: She's lonely. Renée probably never even messaged her. Darcy has glopped on to me because she doesn't really have anybody else. The shadow passes and Darcy perks up, but she knows I've seen it.

"Okay, Darcy, I guess I can camp out at the punch bowl and watch you spin around the room with Arden Kells. I'll ask my mom to drive us."

"And my stepdad will pick us up. He's usually awake till ten."

"Your parents are divorced? Mine, too."

"Is there *anybody* left on the planet who has the same two parents they started with, living under the same roof?"

I could tell her that Evvie and Melissa both do, but she's already off on another subject. I'm really trying to like her. It's not as though I have a dozen other girls crowded around me to sweep me into their circle.

Darcy's waving the lollipop and jabbering on about something, and I interrupt her. "The first day, last week, you talked about Emily Smythe, who used to live in my house."

Darcy drops her backpack to the floor with a thud and does this thing with her hands opening and closing a little door on a clock. "Cuckoo! Cuckoo!" she sings each time her hands open.

"I know." Darcy is so irritating and bossy, but she might know something I need to hear. "Besides Emily being a little off the wall, tell me other stuff about her."

"She has Rapunzel hair, straw blond, down to her waist. She sits on it. Wouldn't that hurt? And really cool clothes, I mean, like, imported, not the usual Old Navy stuff. She has a horse, too. Musta cost thousands of dollars. Her mother used to pick her up in a midnight-blue Maserati. I swear, money leaks out of every pore of that girl."

I think Darcy's envious of Emily, crazy or not.

"Her eyes," Darcy continues, her own face twisted in thought. "There's a look like something awful lurks behind those baby blues. Her locker was two down from mine. Once she slammed it so hard that the clock fell off the wall. She was one angry chicklet."

All that's interesting, but I can tell that something else bothers her about Emily. Again, a hunch, and thinking with my tongue: "Did Arden Kells like her?"

"No accounting for some people's taste," Darcy snaps, frowning. She kicks her backpack into a position so she can pick it up without bending much. "*Ciao, signorina* — that's Italian. Catch you in Language Arts," she says, then sticks the Tootsie Pop back in her mouth and slides into the crowd.

I can learn to like her, maybe. Gotta think about it. But would I have liked Emily Smythe?

Not. A. Chance.

CHAPTER TWENTY-SIX

"MORE SOUP?" MOM ASKS HOPEFULLY. SHE'S GOT about a vat of mushroom barley on the stove, and I do *not* love mushrooms. Or barley. Or soup. Brian hands his bowl over for a refill. No wonder he's Mom's favorite. She brings him an overflowing bowl that splashes onto the saucer, and she sits beside him. "By the way, I had a clock repairman out here today. That stubborn grandfather clock upstairs is fixed. It's only going to say five o'clock when it's five o'clock!"

She sounds so chipper that I get suspicious. I know I'm right as soon as Mom lowers her eyes and says, "Kids, let's talk about Thanksgiving." Now her voice sounds strained, so it must be about Dad.

My back's up, like Terpsichore's when she's around Chester. "Thanksgiving's more than two months away. Why do we have to talk about it now?" I sigh one of those deep, silent ones that shout *Why do you have to make everything so hard?*

But the words that come out of Mom's mouth are cool and calm. "Your father wants to take you two to Chicago to spend the holiday with Uncle Garrett and Aunt Fran."

"All right!" Brian says.

"Just Dad, or does this include Terri and Marcus?"

"The whole family," Mom says, putting on a brittle smile.

"Not me."

"Shelby, be reasonable."

"Who's gonna be here for Thanksgiving?" Brian asks. "You can't eat a whole turkey by yourself."

Mom looks so sad that it almost makes me ask for seconds of soup. "I have a great idea, Mom. Brian can go to Chicago, and I'll stay home with you."

"That's nice of you, Shelby, but it's not possible. The . . . agreement" — she always leaves out the hot word, *divorce* — "says that Dad gets Thanksgiving this year, I get it next year, and so on."

"And so on and so on and so on," I snarl, throwing my spoon down on the table and storming out of the room. Too bad the door to the dining room is a swinging one. I can't slam it, but I make sure it hits the wall and bounces a few times.

"Come here, angry girl, come, come closer." I hear a chorus of quiet voices as I glare at the row of dolls in the hutch. Didn't they used to be lined up in a different order? Mom must have dusted. Or could they have rearranged themselves?

"Where is Baby Daisy?" one of the dolls demands. I'm not sure whose voice I'm hearing. "You must bring Baby Daisy back to us."

Yes, I know she belongs with them, not me, and not with those shattered dolls heaped in the basement of the abandoned house.

Mr. Caliberti said that Betsy Anne, the one with the perky magenta ribbon and sweet smile, represented Sadie's better side. I'm beginning to think I don't have a better side. I'm blunt and irritable and jealous and, well, just plain angry. A lot. I unlock the hutch and take Betsy Anne out. She's warm in my hand. "What do you know that I don't?" I whisper, putting her back with her friends. There's Dotty Woman, who may have poisoned Sadie, and C.B., the Caliberti doll in his knee pants and sailor hat. Miss Amelia's hair is a tangled mess. She looks ragged and weary, as if she never gets enough sleep. They all seem harmless. And yet, Sadie and Emily said they were evil dolls, and Emily buried them in the doll graveyard.

Which they got out of, over and over again.

Where is Lady?

All their eyes are locked on me. In my mind, I hear their pleas and their threats of revenge. Quickly, I stash them back in the hutch, next to that weird pipe Aunt Amelia gave Brian, which Mom thought was so beautiful that it should be displayed for everyone to see. Not that anyone comes way out here. I don't even bother standing the dolls up. When I lock the hutch, I give them one last glance. They're just piled together, like the large, broken dolls in the house up the hill.

Mom and I have sort of made our peace and are perched on two different green velvet couches. At least we can both be in the same room, the ugly parlor, without being snippy (me) or sighing pitifully (Mom). She's crocheting a pot holder in SerenaStockPot.com signature colors, red and purple. She's done about twenty already and plans to put one in each mail-order package. If she ever gets an order.

Brian's upstairs with Mom's laptop, playing chess against some famous chess pro, and Chester's curled in front of the roaring fire, probably deep in a doggy dreamland of meaty bones. Everyone's cozy-content but me.

I've zoomed ahead in *The Giver*, still racking my brain for an A-plus project, but as usual, my mind's wandering and spinning. The dance Friday night. Emily at the mental hospital. Darcy — is she going to turn out to be a friend? What's going on in Grandmother Truva's head? Where's Lady? Dad and Thanksgiving in Chicago. The broken dolls. Revenge. I gaze into the flames, searching for answers and comfort.

Just then, a cinder flies out of the fireplace and singes the rug at my feet. For a split second I freeze, watching a hole expand, then I lurch into action. Forgetting that I'm barefooted, I stomp out the trail of fire that's eating through the carpet. Searing pain seizes the sole of my foot! I hop around on the other foot, shocked to see that the cinder has burst into flame, and the carpet is disappearing before my eyes. I jump away, onto the uncarpeted floor. Mom bats at the flames with a magazine, which ignites, so she hurls the blazing paper into the hearth and picks up a couch cushion to snuff out the fire. That only sends the flames vaulting higher. Chester is leaping on and off the couches, howling like a wolf, a sound I never want to hear again in my whole life.

Through Chester's wails and the crackling flames, I dimly hear Mom yelling, "Get out, get out!"

The heat is at my back like a mean sunburn, so hot, so hot, and the flames are leaping across the parlor, nipping at the corner of the foxhunting tapestry, and I know I have to get out of here *now*, because the whole room's turned orange; I can see it even through my closed eyelids. How could it happen so fast?

"Shelby! Out of the house. Run down the driveway!" Mom hollers, and Chester locks his teeth around my shirt to drag me away. Mom backs off from the blaze and jabs at her cell phone for 9-1-1, waving Chester and me toward the door as the fire nearly reaches the height of the mantel. The wooden mantel will burn like kindling!

But for some strange reason, the fire dies right there, even though a second ago, the room was engulfed in flames. And now everything is smoldering, smelling like burned toast.

Mom shouts, "Shelby Constance, get out of the house this instant. It could all catch again in a flash." She dashes out the door, motioning for me to follow.

I'm petrified. Fire's always been my scariest fear, but I suddenly remember my brother, and I'm hurtling up the stairs.

Chester's running up and down them, confused about what to do.

"Brian!" I shout. "The house is on fire!"

He stumbles out of his room in his pajamas. Panic sweeps across his face when he smells the smoke. I grab his arm, and we tumble down the stairs, Chester behind, herding us out the door like a sheepdog.

Mom's frantically looking for us. As we pour out of the house, she wraps an arm around each of us. "Thank God! I didn't know where you were."

"We're right here, Mom," Brian assures her. "Chester, too."

The fire truck careens into our driveway. How'd they get here so fast? We can see flames jutting wildly again in the parlor window as a fireman asks, "Anybody inside? People? Pets?"

I can barely shake my head. Both my arms are locked around myself, holding me together as if I might burst open and spill my insides. And my burned foot's killing me.

"Door locked?"

No, again. My arms are so tight that my fingers are going numb.

"Run down the driveway," the firefighter commands as he lugs the hose off the rack, zooms into the house, and blasts our front room with water stored in the truck.

It's freezing outside, and Mom's shaking like a tree in a storm. Her teeth are chattering, and she's clasping her hands open and closed. "Mr. Caliberti! Oh, I have to go get him in case the flames leap to his place. You two, stay right there. DON'T MOVE! Chester, keep an eye on them." She runs behind the house to Mr. Caliberti's cottage.

Rubbing my arms to keep warm, I've stepped so far away from our house that I can clearly see the other two houses up the hill, swept bright in the dark night by the headlights of the fire truck.

Mom comes around the house with Mr. Caliberti in his red, ankle-length nightshirt. Terpsichore and Chester are having a standoff, the cat hissing and Chester growling low and ugly. Brian holds Chester's collar, afraid he'll pounce and turn the cat into a midnight snack.

Finally, the fire's still hissing, but the flames have died off for good. Most of our parlor is ruined, and the firemen have carried the three green velvet couches and all the pillows out to the trash, soggy stuffing dangling out of everything.

One fireman says, "I've radioed a disaster service. They'll be out within the hour to set up a wet vac and industrial dryers for your carpet, Mrs. Tate. Be okay in no time."

It'll never be okay as long as we live in this house. My knees are knocking and my heart's going a mile a minute. We came *so* close to broiling in that fire. What if Brian had been in a deep sleep? What if we'd all been upstairs and didn't see the fire starting to leap? We could be totally charred, left as ashes.

I have a sick, nagging feeling about how the fire started, how the cinder leaped out of the fireplace and lit up at our feet, but I don't dare tell Mom.

"Thank you, thank you," we all murmur over and over as the firefighters jump onto their truck and pull away. Trudging up the front steps, Mom says, "I'm grateful that we're all safe. Furniture can be replaced. People can't. Do you want to stay with us tonight, Mr. Caliberti?"

"Kind of you, but Terpsichore and I shall exit stage right and repair to our humble abode. As the great Bard of Avon once wrote, 'O for a Muse of fire, that would ascend / The brightest heaven of invention, / A king-dom for a stage, princes to act / And monarchs to behold the swelling scene!'"

"You got *that* right!" Brian says with a bright, silly grin.

Mr. Caliberti lays his hand on Mom's cheek and whispers, "I always knew Amelia's kith and kin would be lovely people," and he ambles slowly to his cottage with the cat at his side.

Inside, the house smells sharp and bitter, and our feet squish through what's left of the carpet in the par-lor. Only two things in the room seem to have escaped the fire. One's the snap-on chess table and the other's the portrait of Mrs. Thornewood, which I'd have been happy to see changed into kindling.

I spot a third thing that survived. It's the size of a jawbreaker in a puddle where a couch once stood to cover it. A doll's head. I snatch it up before Mom sees it and stuff it in my jeans pocket.

"Can I go back to bed?" Brian asks, rubbing his eyes with the corners of his two index fingers.

"Sure, sweetie," replies Mom. "I'll wait down here for the dryers and I'll turn on all the fans to air out the smoky house. You two go on up. Just open all the windows upstairs and cuddle under lots of blankets."

Chester follows us up the stairs. The grandfather clock in the hall strikes five again. Ha! Mom said it was fixed. I drop Brian and Chester in his room and head for the first-aid kit in the bathroom to soothe my charred foot. Ointment and a thick bandage will help, plus sweat socks and sneakers. So, when I'm sure Chester and Brian are tucked away in his room, I head for the attic, because I've got one of my terrible hunches.

And I'm so right. In the dollhouse, the three green velvet couches that match our ruined parlor ones are gone. No trace of them anywhere. I douse the flashlight and sink against the wall across from the little porthole window, trying to figure out how this might have happened so quickly.

A blast of headlights tells me the disaster fix-it people have arrived with a big truck. They're hauling heavy equipment into the house and quickly set the dryers roaring. Nobody's going to be able to sleep through this. But a great idea strikes me. Now's my chance while there's good light and lots of commotion. Mom won't notice me missing. I tiptoe down the stairs. Mom's got her back to me, standing in the ruined, squishy parlor with two men and four roaring dryers. I slip out the back door and dash up the hill to rescue Baby Daisy.

This time I won't get caught.

CHAPTER TWENTY-SEVEN

THE BASEMENT WINDOW SLIDES UP MORE EASILY
this time, almost as if it's been oiled. I shimmy down the
inside wall instead of jumping and jolting my knees. One
foot lands on something soft. I leap away to solid ground.
Something sweeps across my hair. Ugh. I spin away from
it, relieved to see that it's only the dangling pull-string of
a lightbulb. Pull it, or not? With the blaring lights of the
truck down at our house, no one would really notice if I
turned the light on for a second. I yank the string, and
dim blue light barely makes the mess on the floor visible.
All the dolls and broken parts I'd so faithfully covered
are strewn across the floor. The tarp I'd laid across them
is flung over the banister.

Someone's been here.

Kneeling on the cold cement, I sift through the limbs
and heads, searching for Baby Daisy more by feel than by
sight, but nothing that tiny is among the scattered parts

of these large, soft dolls. So I might as well not take the chance with the light any longer. It zaps off and leaves me in pitch-black again, which is almost better than the bulb that made my skin look a sickly blue.

Footsteps! Someone's in the room right above my head! Terror rockets through me. I grab the tarp, as if it could protect me from whatever lurks in the dark. It's better than nothing. The door at the top of the stairs creaks open. I'm a frozen statue, holding my breath, praying to be invisible in the impenetrable darkness.

A figure slowly creeps down, one step at a time. Closer. Closer. I don't dare step back, but if he gets any closer he'll collide with me. How stupid could I be to sneak into this house?

Two more stairs and we'll be eye to eye. He's taller than I am; I can tell by the movement of air, though I can barely see an outline of a human form. Only one thing to do. I have the advantage of surprise. Quick as a flash, I raise the tarp and throw it over the intruder and bring him crashing to the floor, me on top with the full force of my weight.

"Ouch, you're killing me!" the person under me cries. A girl. She's kicking and thrashing around, and I roll off onto a padding of doll parts.

Mariah throws off the tarp. "Sheesh, you scared the living daylights out of me!"

"What are you doing here?" I shout.

"Could ask you the same thing."

"You first." I get up to pull the light. At least, if we're going to have this ridiculous conversation on the basement floor, we might as well be able to see each other.

"I'm looking for something," Mariah says.

"That makes two of us. Like what?"

She waits a good long time before she admits it. "The journal."

I fake ignorance. "What journal?"

"Sadie and Emily's."

My face always gives me away, and Mariah catches on. "You found it already, right?"

I nod.

"Give it to me."

"It's not yours."

"Not yours, either," Mariah says.

"Is too. It came with my aunt's house."

Mariah's face flashes surprise. "You mean it was never here, in this house?"

"Maybe." Better be cautious.

"That's not what Emily told me. She said she stowed everything away, hid the evidence over here, not in the Thornewood house."

"I guess she lied to you," I say smugly. "Anyway, why do you want the notebook?"

"None of your business," Mariah huffs.

"It's my business absolutely. And I've read every word. Nearly."

"About Sadie?"

"A little about her," I reply.

"About how she died?"

Should I continue to fake it? Might as well be honest. "Not really."

"Phew, that's a relief," Mariah says, hugging herself against the chilling air. "I was afraid —"

"That there was something in the diary about your grandmother?"

"What do you know about my grandmother?" Mariah snaps.

"Well, if you really want to know the truth, there's nothing in the journal that says your grandmother Truva poisoned Sadie, just in case that's what you're worried about."

Mariah gives me one of her classic shrugs, her face now expressionless in the dim blue light. "Who's worried?"

"This place smells moldy. Let's get out of here."

She scrambles to her feet. "But you didn't tell me what you were looking for."

"Doesn't matter," I reply, though my beating heart knows it matters a whole lot.

She shoves her hand into her jeans pocket and pulls out a fist closed around some small object. "Could it be this?" With her other hand she dramatically opens her locked fingers one by one, and there, nesting in her palm, is Baby Daisy.

I snatch her up and tuck her under my friendship bracelet.

Without another word, we each climb out the window and walk carefully toward my house, picking our way through the dark and brush.

"Saw the fire engine. Sorry. Did the fire burn up much in your house?" Mariah asks.

"Just in that stuffy old parlor. I think the high-pressure water did more damage than the flames and smoke, actually."

Neither of us says anything as we get closer to the disaster-service truck, until Mariah cracks the night's quiet: "I'll tell Grandmother Truva she's off the hook."

"Also tell her that her old friend Canto Caliberti says hello. I may bring him down to visit next week."

"Yeah, I'll tell her, but who knows how much gets through the cotton in her brain? Oh, well, we all gotta get old someday, right?"

"Thanks for rescuing Baby Daisy," I whisper.

"Just didn't seem right, her being down there with those busted-up dolls. She needs to be back where she belongs, don't you think? In the doll graveyard." And with that, Mariah takes off running to the main road.

In the morning when I wake up, the house reeks of smoke. Wish I could skip school, but Mom wouldn't let me. She's got breakfast ready out on the cold sunporch, where the windows are open against the burn smell, and where it's a little bit sheltered from the dryers that roar as loud as an airplane engine.

The phone rings. "Who'd be calling at seven in the

morning?" Mom asks, jumping up to answer. She comes back and hands me the phone. "Your friend Darcy," she says, obviously irritated that she'd call so early.

"Hi, Darcy."

"Omygawd, I heard your house was on fire, Shel!"

I wince at the name that only Dad uses. "Just the front room."

"That is so awesomely exciting! Can I come over after school and see the damage?"

Is she totally insensitive? "Sorry, I have a dentist appointment after school."

Mom raises an eyebrow at my little lie.

One bite of my Cheerios and I've decided two things: First, I'm not going to the dance Friday night, no matter what Darcy says. And second, late-breaking bulletin just in: I don't like Darcy even a little bit. With her, every single thing is all about Darcy. So she and Arden Kells can go jump off the nearest cliff holding hands.

CHAPTER TWENTY-EIGHT

"THE INSURANCE ADJUSTER WAS OUT HERE TODAY," Mom tells us at dinner. For once, we're having hamburgers and fries and carrot sticks, like a normal family. "With good news. The insurance will cover most of the damage to the parlor. We'll get a new hardwood floor and carpeting, and we'll replace those ghastly green couches. I'm thinking a nice, soft, cream-colored couch and a small coffee table with shelves for books."

I look up, my hamburger halfway to my mouth. This is the first time I've thought about those dolls under the glass top of the coffee table. They're gone, burned. I wonder if they suffered in the fire. No, of course not, how ridiculous to think so. Especially if it's the dolls that caused the fire, which I suspect.

"Oh, by the way," Mom says, "one of the disaster people found this under a pile of shattered glass from the coffee table. It's amazing this didn't burn up with everything else." She takes a small doll out of her apron pocket and sets it down in front of my plate. I feel all the color drain from my face.

Brian scoots down to get a good look at the doll and announces, "She looks just like Shelby."

I snatch her away, not willing to admit to anyone else that I have a me-doll, just like Emily.

"Hmm. I don't see the resemblance," says Mom. "Oh, and more good news, kids. I got my first customer today. Some lady ordered three different kinds of soup to try for her diner in Santa Fe. Keep your fingers crossed. It could be giant for us."

Brian's not really paying attention. He's probably making chess moves in his head, as usual. All we hear is the *crunch, crunch* of the French fries, when suddenly Brian asks, "Did Aunt Amelia play chess?"

"That last day at the hospital, didn't she say she never took to the game?" Mom asks. "There are lots of things I didn't know about her. Like her romance with Mr. Caliberti. And for the life of me, I still can't picture her smoking a pipe."

"That's what I'm talking about. Why did Aunt Amelia give me that weird pipe?"

We're both startled as he shoves his chair back and runs into the dining room to unlock the hutch. Again I think, *Don't let the dolls out!*

He comes back to the table with the pipe awkwardly dangling from his hand, the tassel brushing his hamburger. He clunks the pipe's porcelain bowl on the table, loosening something rattly.

"Hand it over," I say automatically, but he won't. The bowl is hinged, and he tries to open it with his stubby, nail-bitten fingers. It won't budge. He picks up a knife, licks the mustard off, and uses the end to pry open the cap of the pipe bowl. Mom and I both watch to see what he'll find inside.

"It's probably just dried-up tobacco," I mutter.

"Hunh-uh. Aunt Amelia said it wasn't a smoking pipe." Finally, the knife pries the top open, and it goes flying across the kitchen. Chester thinks it's a game of fetch, and he brings it back. All he gets is a quick head-ruffling, because we're much more interested in the object inside the pipe.

The missing queen.

Brian and I dash into the disastrous parlor, Mom cluelessly trailing us, so Brian can put the queen in her opening spot on the chessboard. She doesn't slide onto the peg easily. He has to twist and jiggle her until she snaps into place with a rewarding *click*.

There's another noise I can't identify for a few seconds until Mom cries, "Look!"

Above the charred mantel, the portrait of Lady Thornewood is sliding to its left, revealing a small square door leading to . . . what?

"Brian, go get the ladder, quick." Mom says, and he flies past us to the garage. Mom tries to reach the silvery, square doorknob in the center of the black door, but her stretched fingers are still inches away. Discouraged, she says, "Our old aunt was full of secrets, wasn't she?"

Which reminds me of something that Aunt Amelia said about Isabella: "We all need friends in high places." This odd little door is sure up high.

The ladder makes a clattery sound as Brian drags it into the room and locks it into position in front of the portrait. I start to climb up the first rung, but Mom shakes her head.

"If anyone's going to break her neck, it'll be me. Stand clear, kids, because who knows what's inside that wall."

I know. At least, I *think* I know.

While we wait with hearts pounding, she carefully climbs up, steadying herself with both feet on each rung. I'd have run right up all those steps and flung that door open by now. Could she be any slower? Finally she's high enough to grasp the doorknob.

"Here goes." But it won't budge. "I don't want to yank back on it too hard because I'm afraid I might tumble off the ladder."

"Can I try?" Brian asks. She'll never let him, but then I remember that Mom's really scared of heights, and she's probably quivering like Jell-O inside right now. In fact, she's slowly coming down, like it's a mountain, and when she reaches the bottom, her face is pasty white.

I give her a quick hug and say, "Let me do it, Mom," and she nods. Yes! I scramble up the ladder; have to go two rungs higher than Mom to reach the doorknob, and I *do* give it a big yank. Nothing happens. I try turning it, but it's not on any kind of swivel.

"Any ideas?" I ask, looking down at Mom and Brian. Mom's thinking, but Brian's fiddling with the chess set. "Brian, for once in your life, get your mind off chess and work with me on this!"

He ignores me, and here I am on the next-to-the-last rung of a ladder, with my head gently clunking against a secret door *that will not open.*

"Try it now," Brian says, looking up expectantly. "I kinda thought the king might be the key, so I turned him one more notch, which wouldn't go until the queen was locked in place."

And Brian is so right! The doorknob's now jiggly in my hand, and the whole door pulls open easily. It's a narrow little safe just big enough for a doll-sized rocking chair. And tied to the chair is a doll that's maybe a foot tall. Her elegant magenta dress is rumpled and moth-eaten. Tatters of lace hang to the floor. There's a scarf over her mouth, a gag, tied in a knot at the back of her head. Some of her upswept hair hangs in knotty straggles around her face, leaving just barely visible two dark blue eyes, wide and terrified and silently screaming *Help!*

"I found Lady," I announce quietly, before I shout it for all the dolls' ears from one end of Cinder Creek to the other: "I FOUND LADY!"

Grasping the doll, chair and all, I tuck Lady under my arm to start back down the ladder, but my hand slips on the wall that supports the ladder, and the ladder swings backward. Suddenly I'm flying through the air.

CHAPTER TWENTY-NINE

FOR A FEW TERRIFYING SECONDS I SEEM TO BE suspended in midair. Frantic voices all around whisper:

"Watch her! She's got Lady in her arms."

"Yes, for heaven's sake, catch her, catch the girl!"

"All these years, banished . . ."

It's not Mom I hear; it's not Brian.

"Ach, no matter. She's safe and sound as sand now."

"Only so if we catch the girl in time! Come, come, all of you!"

And then I'm floating on heavy air, like a magic-carpet ride. The chair with Lady tied to it seems joined to my body as I flutter to the floor and land softly with Mom's arms around me.

"Are you okay, sweetie?" She's probing for broken bones, sprained ankles, bumps on the head.

I'm in a daze, but I nod that I'm okay. It's just Brian and Mom in the room, but I feel surrounded by other beings, souls, whatever you'd call them. I don't see them, or hear them anymore, but I know they're there. I just don't know if they're looking out for me, or for Lady.

Mom takes Lady and the chair out of my arms, and at that moment, I sense something so strong that I can smell it. Fear? Anxiousness? It's like when you're watching for a tottering tightrope walker to land in the safety net. Mom sets the chair and Lady on top of the chessboard, and all at once I'm overwhelmed with a wave of sweet relief.

Brian pulls me to my feet. It's when my sneakers smash the rough-dried carpet that all the *others*, whoever they are, vanish, real life takes over, and I grasp a scary truth: I've just had an out-of-body experience. Does this happen to people who aren't crazy? I don't know anymore.

Mom's bustling around now, setting things straight. She unties Lady from the chair, loosens her gag, and smooths her taffeta dress over her bodice. Brian's occupied with the chessboard, turning the king and queen counterclockwise so the little door snicks closed and Lady Thornewood's portrait slides back into its usual spot.

Now all the voices are silent, except for Mom's: "You scared me to death, Shelby. All for a silly toy like this?"

She holds up the doll, whose eyelids slide closed, as if she's drifted into a deep, dreamless sleep.

My voice is as wobbly as my legs. "She's not a silly toy, Mom. She's the answer to all the weird stuff happening in this house. She's Sadie's doll, the one that represents her mother, Lady Thornewood."

Brian says, "The doll who never got buried with the rest."

"Yes, I remember digging up the grave and finding it empty," Mom murmurs.

A curious calm settles over me. "I'm sure that Sadie locked her in that secret chamber to punish her mother for loving Baby Daisy but never having any love in her heart for Sadie herself."

"What a terrible thing for a child to do," Mom cries.

Brian says, "Maybe the doll deserved it."

"And the mother, I just can't understand how Lady Thornewood couldn't love both her children to pieces, the way I do. The way your father does," Mom adds soberly.

In the kitchen, we clean Lady up and tuck the loose strands of hair into the bun at the back of her head. She seems relaxed now, eyes fluttering open every so often as if to check if she's still in a safe place. I sit her on the table with her magenta gown fanned out around her like a parachute. Black velvet slippers, each with a magenta bow, peek out from under the dress, and looped around her neck and over one shoulder is a small beaded bag with a golden clasp. I've got to open it, right? But what if it's like a jack-in-the-box, and something awful, a paper snake maybe, is released to leap into my face? I carefully open the clasp. Stuffed inside is a sheer linen handkerchief embroidered with violets.

Mom sniffs the hankie. "Rosewater," she declares. "This doll must have been quite the lady of her time."

I'm more interested in the object under the handkerchief, a small mirror framed in a pink-and-purple mosaic. Holding it up to my face, what I see for a split second steals my breath away — a sea of tiny faces behind me. Suddenly that image fades and it's my face, me, clutching the mirror with trembling hands.

Mom is staring at me. "You okay, Shelby?"

All I can do is nod.

"I'm beginning to think you two kids have been probing the mysteries of this house a lot more than I suspected. I remember Aunt Amelia saying she wanted you to tie up loose ends. What else have you found out? Any more about how poor Sadie died?"

"Maybe poisoned with wildflowers, but I don't think so, and neither does Mr. Caliberti."

Then my genius brother pipes up with something totally unexpected. "Maybe it was the parrot. Maybe Plumy brought some yucky disease from way far away, and Sadie caught it."

Far-fetched idea. But it sends me to Google, and what do you know? There was actually a parrot fever mini-epidemic in the early 1930s.

"Brian Tate, how did you get so smart?" Mom says proudly.

"Years of practice," he replies with a grin.

Meanwhile, I'm thinking it all through: It wasn't the governess, Dotty Woman, and it wasn't Mariah's grandmother Truva who poisoned Sadie Thornewood. It was her very own parrot's deadly germs that did her in. Yes, that had to be it! Now Truva O'Donnell and the dolls can rest in peace. But there's something we have to do to make that happen.

With my me-doll in my pocket, I climb in through the basement window of the abandoned house on the hill one last time. Brian's with me, and we've brought a wheelbarrow lined with a blue flannel blanket.

"Sheesh." The word whooshes out of Brian's lips when he sees the shocking pile of broken dolls. One by one, we gently lay the parts and pieces, heads and bodies, into the wheelbarrow outside and cover them all with another blanket. Neither of us has words to fit this solemn job of wheeling the dolls to the little graveyard, digging one large grave, and burying them all together.

I know now what Mr. Caliberti meant when he said there should have been one more grave that sometimes was occupied, sometimes not. He meant it was for the me-dolls that each of us — Emily and I, and probably Sadie, too — had received from the other dolls. Gently I lay mine into the earth, feeling a piece of me go with her. We shovel soft dirt over them all and plant a marker that says *Loyal Friends.*

CHAPTER THIRTY

SATURDAY, AT HIGH NOON, WE'RE STANDING
solemnly in the doll graveyard. I'm wearing my favorite
seafoam-green dress with the little cap sleeves. I need to
feel the wind, the cold, the mist, and everything else for
this important occasion.

The dolls are warm. All of them, including Isabella,
are wrapped in the red-and-purple pot holders Mom
made, with just their heads showing. But I'm not sure
what we should do with Isabella. Should she be buried
with the rest?

Brian and I lay all the named dolls out on the ground.
Chester sniffs each one, then curls in the center of the
horseshoe. We've dug a new grave for Lady so she can be
closer to the others instead of being banished across the
cemetery. We've made new markers, too, these out of
clay, and etched each doll's name while the clay was

soft. One of them has a large gravestone with this epitaph on it:

Here in this grave lies young Betsy Anne.
The sweetest doll of the whole Thornewood clan.
The best parts of Sadie she carries to heaven.
For the girl sadly perished at the age of eleven.

Mr. Caliberti and Terpsichore are the first to arrive for the funeral. He's wearing a black suit and one of those old-fashioned hats Mom calls a fedora. He sits on his little cane/stool and gazes at the Miss Amelia doll, which Terpsichore is tickling with her whiskers. We've cleaned up Miss Amelia, painted over some of the cracks on her face, and combed her black hair into a sleek mane. She looks almost beautiful, for a witch.

As he leans over and gently toes Miss Amelia, he says ever so sadly, "My dear Amelia simply wouldn't accompany me to the altar."

"Why not?" I ask, helping him straighten up. Mom thinks I'm too nosy and gives me a look that could shrivel me into a prune.

"Ah, we all have our sacred secrets, do we not, people?"

"Tell us what yours is," Brian says, "and then I'll tell you that I cheated in chess once when I beat my dad. Just once, though. He caught me." His face turns red in embarrassment.

"My indiscretion is far worse, young Mr. Brian. You see, I was drafted and ordered to Germany during World War Two. I begged my dear Amelia to marry me at once before a justice of the peace and come abroad with me, but she declined. She wanted a full-stage church wedding with all the fanfare of a coronation."

"Our no-frills Aunt Amelia?" Mom asks in surprise.

"The same. So, as ashamed as I am to say it, I tarried, went AWOL, which is to say, I left my military unit and walked three hundred miles back to Amelia."

Terpsichore is winding herself around and around Mr. Caliberti's legs, as if she knows what's coming next.

"Well, Amelia Stanhope was a girl of highest, uncompromising standards. She simply refused to marry a man who would desert his patriotic duty. Even though later I served on the front for two years, she remained steadfast. Alas, there would be no wedding, church or otherwise."

I have a bunch more questions, but I panic when Mr. Caliberti leans over so far that I'm afraid he'll land on his nose in the middle of the graveyard. Maybe he's fainting!

But no, he's just noticed Isabella for the first time. He picks her up and shucks off her pot-holder cover to reveal her gorgeous golden, bejeweled gown and hat. "This one is *not* to be buried," he says sternly, clutching Isabella to his chest as he settles back on his stool.

"How come?" Brian asks before I can get the same words out of my mouth. My brother, who never used to talk much? Boy, he's making up for it.

"Forgive me, I'm a smidgen dizzy," Mr. Caliberti whispers, his eyes sort of spinning. Terpsichore circles him protectively until he clears his throat to speak. "Mark my words, people, this doll is not like the others."

"Who does she represent?" I ask.

"Whom," he corrects me. "We must be precise in the THEE-uh-tah. Clever young Miss Shelby and young Mr. Brian, have you not figured out who Isabella is?"

I'm scrolling through the whole cast of characters I know from Sadie's time and Emily's time, and I can't come up with a single person Isabella might represent. Yet Aunt Amelia must have thought this doll was important in the mystery of Cinder Creek, or she wouldn't have given me Isabella's floppy golden hat.

Mr. Caliberti asks, "Are you bewildered? Flummoxed? Then I shall tell you, tragic though it is. You see, just as Betsy Anne represents all of Sadie Thornewood's best hidden qualities, Isabella represents Sadie living on into adulthood, grown to a beautiful young woman, even though the poor child knew that she was dying. This she whispered in my ear, handing me Isabella, days before she closed her eyes for the last time."

"Oh . . ." Mom and I cry together.

"You see," Mr. Caliberti continues, "that is why she never meant to bury Isabella, but asked me instead to hide this doll where a worthy person would find her and understand what swelled in Sadie's heart at that moment when her anger turned to hope." He faces me with that same intense look I've seen in his eyes before. "And that is why our dear Amelia arranged for you to grasp the secrets of this house."

Before I can even think about the astonishing thing he's just told us, Mariah arrives, pulling Grandmother Truva behind her. Truva's wearing an ankle-length navy-blue cape with a red silk rose at her throat. Her hair looks like she's just come from the beauty parlor, but her eyes are as lifeless as ever.

Mr. Caliberti gets up off his stool. "Why, Truva O'Donnell, you look as lovely as ever. You haven't aged a day. Come over here. Let me have a better look at you." He takes her by the hand, and for a flash of a minute, her eyes light up as he seats her on his stool and stands unsteadily beside her. Mom moves closer in case he starts to toddle.

Mariah whispers to me, "I explained everything to my grandmother, about the parrot and all. I think she's okay with it now."

Mr. Caliberti asks me to hand him the C.B. doll, his me-doll. He says, " 'Now cracks a noble heart. Good night, sweet prince: And flights of angels sing thee to thy rest!' " And he hands me C.B. to place in his grave.

Mariah raises Betsy Anne, wrapped in red and purple, and turns the doll to face the rest of us. In her usual flat voice, cracking just a little if you listen carefully, Mariah says, "Sorry I never knew this side of Sadie Thornewood, but I'm glad to meet her now." She lays Betsy Anne into her own little grave and sprinkles a handful of dry dirt over her.

Then Grandmother Truva shuffles to her feet and says, "Yea, though I walk through the valley . . ." She stops, all confused, adds "God bless," then retreats into silence again. Mr. Caliberti has looped his arm through hers.

No one knows what to say next. Mom glances around, and when no one speaks up, she says, "I guess it's my turn." Kneeling, she tucks Baby Daisy into her red-and-purple bunting and nestles her into the tiny grave. "Sweet little one, if I'd been your mother, I would have loved you fiercely, and your sister, Sadie, just as much."

Lady is the largest of the dolls, even larger than Isabella. I'm amused to see that Terpsichore and Chester are both dozing, with Isabella sitting between them like a referee.

Brian has a few words to say about Lady as we pour fresh earth over her wrapped body: "Lady Thornewood, thanks a lot for the queen. If I win the chess tournament next month, I'll come and tell you." That gets a tension-bursting laugh, which seems like a good time to bury Dotty Woman. I stand her up in her grave so everyone can see the perpetual wide grin on her playful face.

Mr. Caliberti squints to see her better and says, "Ah, yes, the young thing brought such laughter to a sad and troubled house. Pity there are no dandelions to accompany her on her journey."

There's only one doll left. I kneel beside Mom and motion for Brian to join us. "Miss Amelia, we didn't know you until you were our pipe-smoking old *aunt* Amelia." Mom and Brian both smile. And suddenly I'm choking up, unsure what to say, because my family knows Aunt Amelia wasn't my favorite person on earth. But she gave me a huge, enormous gift, so I say the four most meaningful words that spring to my mind: "Thank you, Aunt Amelia."

All the graves are covered now, each with a marker: *Betsy Anne*, *Miss Amelia*, *Dotty Woman*, *Baby Daisy*, *C.B.*, and *Lady*. Terpsichore wakes up and dances lightly over each grave, with Chester's eyes following her suspiciously. As Mr. Caliberti once said, Terpsichore "trips the light fantastic." And it *has* been fantastic.

Suddenly there's nothing more to say, except "Rest in peace," which we all murmur.

"And leave my children in peace," Mom adds.

The next time Dad comes, I'll bring him out here to see the doll graveyard and tell him all about the funeral.

Tonight, after Mom's asleep, I'm going to find the page that's smack in the middle of the diary and sign in a black Sharpie, *SHELBY TATE WAS HERE*, with the date. Then I'm going to stash it back under the floor at the foot of the stairs. It's the right thing to do, because it belongs to the house. To Sadie Thornewood. To Emily Smythe. Not to me. Then tomorrow I'm going to figure out how to get a phone number for Emily because she deserves to know that the things she saw and heard about the dolls and their mischief really happened, that she's not crazy. And that all the dolls are resting in peace now and the drama's over.

Unless the dollhouse up in the attic has other plans for us. I'll know as soon as I step in the house — if the grandfather clock bongs five o'clock again.

Mom wipes tears out of her eyes and smiles brightly. "Well, who's ready for lunch? A nice big bowl of steamy-hot soup? Chicken noodle or posole, your choice," she offers.

We all head back into the house just as the *America's Most Amazing* van arrives, and the producer guy, Drue What's-His-Name, waves a letter at us and yells out merrily, "Hey, I got clearance from the bank to shoot the

house up there on the hill, woo-hoo! My crack produc-
tion crew'll be along in *uno minuto*."

We all laugh, even Chester, even Terpsichore, maybe
even Grandmother Truva, because it's too late now.

Everything amazing has already happened.

Looking for more haunting stories? Turn the page for a sneak peek at Suzanne Weyn's creepy new series The Haunted Museum!

JESSICA'S BACK WAS TURNED TOWARD SAMANTHA as she searched through the cabin, combing through each of the still-empty dresser drawers.

"Oh, good. You're here," Samantha said. If Jessica was here, it meant she wasn't on the deck with John. "I got so lost trying to find the costume room, but maybe you can help me?"

Samantha stepped inside and saw that Jessica was wearing a black maid's uniform with a white apron and ruffled mobcap. Black stockings and ankle-high boots completed the outfit. Of all the costumes she could have selected, why would she decide to be a maid? It wasn't like Jessica to pick such an unfashionable costume.

"What are you looking for?" Samantha asked as she stepped farther into the cabin.

"The locket! I have to find it!"

Samantha froze. The voice she'd just heard was high and raspy. It wasn't her sister's voice.

The figure turned.

It definitely wasn't Jessica.

Gaping, Samantha stared at the girl she had mistaken for her sister. No more than fifteen, the girl was thin and pretty but with pale skin and deep shadows beneath her dark, burning eyes. Her lips were dry and her hands trembled ever so slightly. Her dark hair hung lifelessly at the sides of her gaunt face.

Samantha couldn't stop staring.

"The locket — you stole it from me."

"What?" Samantha asked. "I didn't steal a locket from anyone. I don't know what you mean." She didn't like being around this girl. Samantha hoped she would leave right away. "Honestly, there's no locket here."

"You're lying," the girl insisted. "I know you are. Give it back to me."

As the girl spoke, her face was changing before Samantha's eyes. It appeared to be contorting into a different shape, shifting into someone — something — else.

"What are you doing?" Samantha asked, her voice a quaking whisper. Although she wanted to look away, she was too amazed to even turn her head.

When the girl replied, her voice dropped to a low growl. "I'm not doing anything."

"But your face," Samantha said, backing away.

"What about my face?" the girl asked in a snarl.

Samantha grabbed the doorknob as she realized what the face was becoming.

A skull!

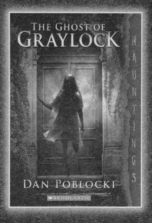